# RAVAGED BY LUST

## (RAVAGED ROCKSTARS II)

### REBECCA CASTLE

ISBN: 9780645587708

# PLAYLIST

These Are The Days - Inhaler
Motion Sickness - Phoebe Bridgers
If You Ever Leave, I'm Coming With You - The Wombats
Love You So Bad - Ezra Furman
Grow Old with Me - Tom Odell
Missing Piece - Vance Joy
Landslide - Fleetwood Mac
I Will Follow You into the Dark - Death Cab for Cutie
Save Your Tears - The Weeknd
I Need My Girl - The National

*I remember all those times*
*Those times I made you laugh and cry*
*We stayed up late, we kissed, we loved*
*Why can't we go back there, baby?*
*Why can't I see that smile?*

# PROLOGUE

## *BISHOP*

"ONE DAY, I'm going to be a rockstar," Chloe whispers to me in between my relentless kisses on her lips. Her announcement, sinking in after coming out of freaking nowhere, makes me pull back from her.

"Oh, really? You're going to be a rockstar?"

"Don't mock me, I'm being serious," she replies with that cute little pout of hers. I simply smile and ruffle her hair with my hand. She absolutely hates it when I do that, and that's precisely why I do it every chance I get.

"And I'm being serious too," I say. "I believe you will be a rockstar, Chloe. I believe you can be whoever the hell you want to be."

She looks at me. *Man.* She is the most fucking beautiful thing I've ever seen. Every time she gazes at me like that with her vibrant green eyes and long black hair, she takes my breath away.

And she doesn't even know that. She doesn't know the

extent she's caught me enthralled by her beauty like a prisoner.

We're sitting on her bed, in her bedroom, and I most definitely should *not* be here. In fact, I think I would actually be killed if I was discovered to be here by none other than Chloe's brother... and my best friend.

As if sensing my thoughts, Chloe starts talking about him.

"I will be a rockstar, Bishop. I feel it in my bones. Music is the one thing that gives me passion."

"Hey, and what about me?"

"And *you*, of course."

"That's better."

"You know that Axel and I are going to start a band together, right?"

*Please let's not talk about him...*

Anything to avoid the best friend I'm currently betraying by being in this room.

"You and your brother?" I ask her.

"Yep. We're going to be a brother and sister band. Kinda like Angus and Julia Stone."

"Or the Jackson Five," I suggest with a snicker.

I lean back to kiss her, but she punches me on the arm.

"No, not them, stupid," she replies, her cute pout returning with a vengeance. "Axel and I, we're going to be *so* cool. A songwriting duo making music that speaks to people's souls. We'll tour everywhere and have millions of fans."

"So," I say with a deep breath. "Let me get this straight... you're saying that you're gonna travel the world with your brother as a famous rock band, touching people's souls or whatever..."

"Yep."

"And where do I picture in all of this?" I ask her. "You

do know that Axel is my best friend, right? He won't be happy if I follow you two around like a lapdog screwing his sister."

"Hey, watch your tongue, mister. You'll be right there alongside us, Bishop. Alongside me. If you want, of course."

She's deadly serious. Sincere about this dream to her bones.

"I somehow doubt that Axel will like the fact that we're together, Chloe. I mean, we're still having to keep all this quiet from him and it's been *months*."

Chloe bites her lip, contemplating. "That is one small problem."

The fact that her brother hasn't found out yet is a goddamn miracle, and I would very much like things to remain that way.

"You think?" I sarcastically question her. "What about the little fact that we're currently hiding in your bedroom from both your brother and your mom? I like Astrid and all, but I don't think she'll be liking me very much if she walked in right now and saw us two here, like this."

Both our eyes flicker to the closed bedroom door. Chloe's family reckons she's just quietly in here doing her homework.

And certainly not kissing her brother's best friend.

"Yep. She wouldn't be so friendly."

"It does throw a spanner in your dream, doesn't it?"

"But what do you think?"

"I've told you what I think. I think you can conquer the world, Chloe."

"Shut up. You're such a joker."

"This time I am being so fucking serious."

"I hate how I have to pretend to not know you properly at school," she says quietly. "How I have to pass you in the hallways and pretend you're not like this with me."

"I find it sexy," I say. "Creeping around. Sneaking through your window."

"I did at the beginning, but it's been months."

*And I hope it's going to be plenty more months.*

I lean towards her. "This is our little secret, though. Isn't that enticing?"

"You're smarter than you look, Bishop. You've convinced the whole town of Crystal River that you're some cool, cocky, confident guy who's a genius at everything he turns his hand to and is a playboy hit with the ladies when you're actually a sweetheart."

"Ew. Don't ever call me that again."

"Hang on," Chloe whispers, placing a shushing finger over my lips.

From the room next door comes the deep resonant sound of a bass guitar being played. Chloe and I freeze, listening to it.

Listening to my best friend practice without a single clue what's going on in his sister's room adjacent to his.

"Well, it's a good thing he didn't hear me climb through your window," I whisper.

"It's a good thing that he's making some noise," Chloe replies.

"Noise? Why?"

She kisses me then. More passionately that the playful ones we've been sharing all night. I feel her hands travel all over me. Down my back. Past the long faint scar on my chest. Towards my pants...

She gets on top of me on the bed, pushing me down on my back aggressively. I don't protest. This is so incredibly sexy. Seeing her take control makes me hard. Her wandering hands start to fumble with my belt, but I take hold of her wrists before she gets too far.

"Are you ready for this?" I ask her in a hushed voice.

"Yes."

"Really ready?"

She nods.

And that's when I know it's time to take her virginity.

"This will be my first time," she says. As if I didn't know.

We're both eighteen. We've both been waiting for this moment for months of our secret courtship.

"And it'll be my first time as well," I reply.

She scoffs. "You're a liar."

"I'm not."

"But you're... *you*, Bishop. You'd have to be an idiot not to know every girl at school fantasizes about you. You're insanely charismatic and cool and sexy and just freaking gorgeous. All the girls flock to you."

"And I've only got eyes for you. How about that?"

"Bishop..."

I know she's nervous. She's talking in an attempt to take her mind off what we're about to do.

I'm the man here. I need to get our focus back.

*I need to seize control.*

"I'll take this slowly," I tell her. "Like a love song."

"Don't be cheesy, Bishop."

I ignore her teasing.

"I want to take care of you, Chloe. Let me lead you."

She nods again, and I see all the anxiety drain from her eyes. I train my gaze on her. Let her understand that there's nothing to be afraid of.

That this is going to be an act of love.

I take her virginity with care, and she takes mine with all the responsibility she has.

As first times go, I imagine this one is pretty special. Sure, there's some fumbling. Some awkward moments. But we're careful with each other. We make each other feel safe. We repeat how we're feeling, and I make sure to check up with Chloe multiple times. Make sure she's okay.

And then it's over.

"Doing that," I whisper in Chloe's ear. "With your brother next door not suspecting a thing was pretty damn sexy."

"Oh, it was. We're very naughty."

"It was beautiful," I say. None of my male friends would ever hear me say something like this in public, but the words feel right to tell Chloe.

It *was* fucking beautiful.

"It's funny," she replies.

I raise an eyebrow. "What's funny?"

"The cool and dashing and confident Bishop Hayes who all the girls love being all sentimental and vulnerable. Yeah, you are definitely a sweetheart."

"I can act hard if you want me to."

"No, I like you like this, Bishop," she says. "It feels like I'm sharing a secret with you; your true side that you hide from the world."

"Well, I can't hide anything from you, Chloe."

She reaches for my hands and interweaves her fingers in mine.

"I'm so used to you having such a dirty mouth that it's weird to hear you talk like this," she observes.

"I loved *fucking* you just then. I loved it when your mouth was around my hard cock. Is that the dirty mouth you were referring to?"

She giggles.

"There's something about me you should know, Chloe."

"What is it?" she asks.

"I never like to lose."

"A competitive guy. I like that."

"I like you," I reply, and Chloe blushes. "And I like it the most when you blush."

We lie opposite each other, staring into each other's eyes for a long time. Basking in the glow of our first time. Chloe holds my hands tight like she doesn't want to let me go.

"I want you to show me something," I eventually say.

Chloe sits up, intrigued. "What do you want me to show you?"

"Going back to your rockstar dream. I know you write songs. I've seen you at school scribbling away on notepads in the back of the class. If you really want to be a musician when you're older, you gotta be writing songs, and you're probably hiding them somewhere. I'll like to see them."

Chloe shakes her head. "No."

"Come on, it'll be my secret."

There's a long pause as she mulls it over. She takes in a deep breath.

"I've actually written a song about you," she says.

"No way."

"Yep."

"Well, now you've got to show me."

"It's a work in progress," she says.

"I don't care. Show it to me."

She reaches into her bedside drawer and takes out a notepad. I recognize the one as the same that she brings to high school every day. The one she doesn't let anyone else look inside.

*So that's what is in it. Songs.*

She flips to a page and then carefully and cautiously hands it over to me.

"Promise you won't laugh at me," she says.

"I would never do that."

"Promise."

"I promise, Chloe. I wouldn't break a promise to you."

I read the whole thing. Once. And then again.

I don't say a word until I'm completely finished. Chloe watches me for my reaction with bated breath. I think I'm the first person she's ever shown her lyrics to.

*It's a fucking big responsibility.*

I close the notepad and look at her dead in the eye.

"Chloe Stoll, I believe one day you *are* going to be a rockstar."

*When I see you,*
*my heart stops beating*
*How can I live*
*when you're right there?*
*All of my fear flies away*
*when you come to me*
*And kiss my lips*

*I've been waiting*
*every day of my life for you*
*Waiting for time to bring us together*
*Now that you're mine, I can't believe*
*That this is forever*

*I will be strong and brave for you*
*Because that's what you deserve*
*Nothing will stand*
*between me and you*
*Our forever we will preserve*

*So come with me and let's see*
*What our forever holds*

# 1

*CHLOE*

IF MY LIFE WERE A MOVIE, it would be a tragic comedy.

You'll start the movie with those typical nostalgia-driven shots of young me playing the guitar and singing into the microphone in my mom's living room with my brother, trying to emulate the musicians I adored. You know those kinds of shots? The ones that are sepia-filtered in every kind of biographical movie? All gold and shining.

That would be my hopeful childhood.

And then, in this movie of my life, the director will suddenly cut to a cold and gray discount department franchise store with a dour adult me standing behind a till getting paid minimum wage. I bet the audience will laugh at that. The contrast between a happy and optimistic childhood and the harsh reality of having to work in some shitty store in my hometown, my dreams unfulfilled.

Yep. A tragic comedy.

*Laugh at my misfortune.*

But who am I kidding? There wouldn't be a movie of

my life. Not in a million years. There might be a movie of my brother's life, that's for sure. I would probably even appear in it, as a fleeting background character in a single scene.

But no movie for me. No movie for the failed sibling to a world famous rockstar.

I'm still into music. That's the one thing that hasn't changed. Axel and I share many things... our green eyes... our stubbornness... our loyalty...

And especially our love of music. It's my dedication. It gives me joy. Whenever I pick up my guitar and start to strum, I feel a sense of purpose that makes everything all good in the world. My minimum-wage job and my minimum-fulfilled life drop away, and I am at peace.

The day I go viral on the internet is the same day my brother's girlfriend gets pregnant, and it is the same day I have a nine-hour shift as a cashier at said discount department franchise store.

*Not exactly the best beginning for a movie of my life.*

There has been a lot that's happened today that it's going to take me a minute to unpack it all.

First, going viral on the *freaking internet...*

I don't actually know that I have gone viral until I'm standing behind that till and see my manager disappear for a sneaky cigarette break.

"I'm going to check the accounts," she tells us.

*Sure.*

Karen, my manager, has made it her New Year's resolution to quit smoking and has decided to make it pretty public in my hometown of Crystal River exactly what she was doing. Hence why she tiptoes off outside at the back by the dumpsters every hour to spend a squirreled-away five minutes puffing away. *Checking the accounts.*

She thinks she's being so secretive, but everyone in

Crystal River knows it. Small town gossip flies around fast. But the good thing is that when she does sneak off, us employees are granted a few precious minutes to take a little impromptu break ourselves without Karen's beady eyes on the camera monitors. We grab something quick to eat, sit down for a bit, read a magazine. Anything to momentarily escape the dullness of our minimum-wage job.

Over the years, I've gone from the wild-eyed optimist of my teenage youth into someone my mother likes to call a cynic.

This particular time Karen's gone out back for her little unofficial break I mindlessly check my phone, expecting the usual deluge of spam emails and your average Monday's dry social media feed, but what I didn't expect was for the video I quickly uploaded online late last night to have nearly a million views.

I mean, I can literally *see* the view count rise up and up as I stare at my phone in sheer disbelief.

*What the hell...*

956,100...

957,341...

958,287...

Rising and rising every freaking second.

The video is a song that I wrote. It's just me in it. Me in my bedroom. Performing with my guitar in front of my crappy little webcam.

*Surely this is a mistake.*

A million views. And growing. This is definitely not a drill.

*Holy shit.*

I've been posting videos of my songs online for years - for nearly a whole damn decade – but barely anyone has watched them. I've been considering a few hundred hits on a video as a success.

But this video from last night? It turns out some influencer shared it, and then another did, then another, then some big music influencer. All within the space of a morning I'm rapidly seemingly on the front page of every social media platform. All while I've been standing behind a till.

"Get off your phone, Chloe."

Ah, it's Karen. Back from her little break, and she's already bearing down on us like a managerial eagle.

"I'll dock a formal complaint if I see you on it again, Chloe. Back to work."

"Okay, Karen."

I put my phone away, but then I just stand there behind the till. In shock. I ignore the next customer until they wander off to the next till.

*A million fucking views.*

It can't be real.

But it is. I saw that number with my own eyes. A million people all over the world have watched me sing a song that I wrote in the space of a few hours.

Finally, *something* has happened with my passion, and now my hands are trembling and I don't know what to do and... Oh God, this has all come at once and it's freaking me the freak out.

I feel the vibration of my phone on the counter in front of me. I'm starting to get messages.

*I better check these. I better do... something.*

And so I head to the restroom. It's the only excuse where I can sit down and actually be on my phone without Karen glowering over me like she will definitely do if I stayed at the till. I just have to see this all again. I just have to show myself that I have actually gone viral.

985,345...

986,169...

I scroll through my phone in shock. There are messages from strangers. Complete strangers who congratulate me and give me compliments that just fly over my head. People trying to get in touch with me to do paid advertising. Trolls as well, but I ignore them.

So.

Many.

People.

They're all watching and commentating on something that I'm doing. Something I love.

I just scroll and scroll and scroll and scroll.

It seems like my family hasn't noticed this at all yet. There are no messages from Axel or my mom.

990,351...

991,194...

I spend ten minutes just sitting there on the toilet with my phone in my hands.

Until there's a knock on the door.

It's Karen. Of course it's freaking Karen.

"Chloe? You've been in there for a long time, longer than you're allotted for under your work conditions. Back on the tills."

I try to take in a deep breath. And then another. I summon up the will to put my phone down and get back to work.

*I'll just have to deal with all this craziness when I finish my long-ass shift.*

And so I make my way back to my position.

And then, as I'm strolling through the store, my phone rings. It just rings in my hands. A number that I don't recognize.

I feel like this must be connected to all of this.

"Hello?"

"Am I talking to Chloe Stoll?"

It's the biggest producer of music in North America. Mickey Miller of Miller Records. Producer of some of the most famous stars in music for the last forty years.

He's the one calling me.

Well, *technically,* his assistant is. I don't know how Miller Records even got my phone number, but I don't care.

"I'm glad we've been able to reach you. I've got some news to share with you," she says.

The assistant and I talk for a moment. Apparently, the producer has come across my video. How quick of him. I guess it *is* his job.

"Chloe, get off your phone." Karen has snuck up behind me. Her sharp voice rings in my ears. "How many times do I have to ask you? I'll write you up for this."

I mute my phone and spin around to my manager. She glares at me with such indignation.

"If you're allowed a made-up cigarette break every hour, Karen, then I can have one life-changing phone call."

That shuts her up. I return to my phone call.

"As I was saying," the assistant continues. "Mr. Miller would like to schedule a meeting. When are you next in Los Angeles?"

My mouth goes dry. I don't say a word. I can't go to LA; I'm dead broke. I'm always dead broke. I might have to borrow money from god-knows-who to even get to LA. Besides, it's not my favorite city in the world.

*But Mickey Miller wants to meet me?*

Even I'm not dumb enough to realize this truly is a once-in-a-lifetime opportunity.

"I'll be there in the next few days. I can send you my details?"

"Message me on this phone number. I'll arrange the meeting."

And then the assistant hangs up, and I feel a wave of power flow through me.

*Is this really happening?*

I turn around again. Karen is still staring at me.

"Give me your phone, Chloe," she barks. "I'm confiscating it until the end of your shift, and I'm docking your wage for this hour."

I just laugh then.

I don't give her my phone. Instead, I take off my name badge and place that into my manager's open hand.

"I quit, Karen. Enjoy your cigarettes. Everyone knows about it."

And then I pick up my bag from under the counter and walk out of that shitty store and the job I hate.

I'm overwhelmed with nervousness, but I don't let that show as I stroll to my car on the other side of the parking lot.

It's only when I sit in the driver's seat that I let out the longest sigh of my life.

"What have you done, Chloe?" I ask myself.

For once I'm taking a risk – the biggest freaking risk of my life - and I'm running with it. *That's* what I'm doing.

I've somehow become viral.

I shake my head. This is unbelievable.

*Impossible.*

Still shaking my head, I start up my car, and then my phone rings again. This is a number I do recognize.

Axel Stoll.

My brother.

"Guess what?" I ask him as I pick up. "You wouldn't believe what's happened today..."

But he interrupts me.

"Chloe, Maddie is pregnant."

His words cut straight through mine.

And now we come to the second crazy part of today.

"Maddie? Your new girlfriend I haven't met yet?"

"You've had chances to meet her, Chloe."

"Sorry, but work has been insane. I've followed your whirlwind romance on the news, though. You're saying she's pregnant? Like, for real?"

"Yes, for real. For real. You're going to be an auntie, Chloe."

"Holy shit, Axel. Congratulations."

"And we'll love for you to come and see us in LA. It will be nice for you to come out here, even though I know you don't like the place."

Ha.

What a fucking coincidence.

*L-freaking-A. City of Angels.*

Meet Mickey Miller and meet my nephew-niece.

"Yes. I'm coming, Axel," I reply. "Try and stop me."

# 2

*CHLOE*

"You must be Chloe, I'm Maddie. It's lovely to meet you finally."

The short girl with light brown hair and soft blue eyes who greets me at the front door of Axel's place is the very epitome of warmth. Her smile lights me up on the spot and makes me instantly forget the long-ass day of traveling on a crowded flight across the country I've just endured.

"I'm Chloe," I reply, offering out my hand.

Maddie looks down at my hand with a dismissive smirk. "Let's not do formality, Chloe. Come on in for a hug, we're practically sisters now."

I laugh and we embrace affectionately.

"It's so good to finally meet you," I say. "I mean, God, a woman that Axel's *actually* falling in love with? Seemingly impossible. I've got to pick your brains and find out who the hell you are and how on earth you transformed my stupid brother."

Maddie blushes. "Sure..."

"Sorry," I say, sensing her bashfulness. "I can be quite... *loud.*"

"Just like Axel," Maddie replies with a chuckle. "It certainly runs in the family, but that's why I love him."

I didn't know who I was expecting when I came out here, but Maddie definitely isn't what I would have in mind. With her cute blushing and shy demeanor, I can already deduce that she's the polar opposite to my cocky, brash, free-spirit brother. Maybe it's why they work so well together.

"Can I take your bags?" Maddie asks, nodding at the luggage I've wheeled behind. I have my trusty old guitar on my back as well.

"I'm fine, I'm fine. You're the pregnant one here. I can bring in my own stuff."

Maddie laughs again. "I've been pregnant for basically two minutes, so please don't treat me like I'm about to give birth. I'll show you inside. Your brother is somewhere in here. Probably practicing his guitar instead of greeting his sister he hasn't seen for a long time."

I follow Maddie inside her place. It's beautiful in here; she and Axel have really made a home for themselves. A place fit for a family one day. This house is, by far, the best purchase I can say Axel's made with his rockstar money. It's much more sensible – and safer – than the crazy vintage motorbike he got when he signed his first record deal.

"So, you've got to tell me how you two actually met," I say to my brother's girlfriend as she guides me inside.

"What? Axel hasn't told you?"

"Nope. I mean, I've seen the news and know that whole *mainstream media* narrative of you two and your very public romance..."

Maddie rolls her eyes.

"God, I'm beginning to really despise journalists," she

comments as she ushers me down the hallway into their large living room. There's an entire array of Axel's guitars hanging decoratively on the walls. That man and his expensive toys. Like that dangerous motorbike of his, he has always been into splashing money on trying to look cool. I bet he's built up a really nice car collection as well, the bastard. "It's so weird reading about yourself online and not recognizing yourself at all."

"How did you two actually meet then?" I ask. "The *real-life* version and not the tabloid one? I want to know."

"It's been kind of a secret."

I raise my eyebrow. "Oh, yeah? Do tell me more."

"Well, it was technically a *fake* relationship."

"Fake? No freaking way."

She shrugs.

"He was the party playboy, and I was the girl who was hired to reshape his image," Maddie explains. "It was just meant to be a fake thing for a few weeks to boost the sales for Ravaged's new album but, well, things got a bit more... *heated* than we bargained for."

"Oh, I see. Spicy."

"But we're still keeping that a secret from the world," she continues. "Look, I'm only telling you because you're family, but not many people know about how things started between Axel and me, and we'll like to keep it that way. To be honest, I really disliked the guy at first. I thought he was arrogant and cocky."

"You ain't telling me anything new," I reply with a smirk. "I had to grow up with the ass."

"He was certainly not my type of man at all," Maddie says, grinning at my comment. "But then, as I got to know him, things started to change. I saw the real him."

Even though he's my brother and I would love every

opportunity to punch his snide little face, my heart does melt at how lovingly Maddie talks about him. I've always known, deep down, that Axel was a true little romantic softie. Years of being a playboy rockstar just clouded that from view. And it seems like Maddie's been the girl to mine it out of him.

"You're divine," I say to her. "I like you already, and I can see what my brother sees in you. To be honest, though, I think you're too good for his sorry ass."

Maddie blushes. "You're sweet, Chloe."

"It's the truth. That man doesn't deserve you."

"You know that you two look so alike," Maddie remarks, staring at me. "Especially your green eyes. Your mom, Astrid, has the same as well."

I shake my head.

"The famous Stoll green eyes. We can't seem to get rid of them. Maybe that little baby growing inside you might get that trait too. Congratulations, by the way. I don't think I've said that yet."

Maddie smiles and rubs her tummy. "I can't believe I'm actually pregnant. It came as a complete shock. I wasn't feeling well for a few days and thought I would take a test, just to be sure, and then..."

"Yeah, trust me, when Axel called telling me... it came as quite a shock to me too. My crazy older brother has actually found a beautiful girl and got her pregnant? I bet pigs can fly now as well."

"Shall I give you a quick tour of the place?" Maddie asks me. "Who knows? We might even find Axel in here somewhere."

"Sure."

I drop off my bags in the living room and my brother's girlfriend shows me their new home. It's so expansive. As she takes me around, she informs me that Axel just bought it a few months ago. It's got all the features a family needs; there's a pool and everything. I like the kitchen most of all; it's exactly the same type I dream of having one day. Minimalistic, but homely. Maddie tells me it's her dream kitchen. She seems so happy. So content. Both she and Axel have found true love, it seems. Great for them. I may be the annoying man's sister, but even I can admit that they deserve this happy life.

*Axel's done good.*

"Are you still working?" I ask Maddie. "Mom said something about you being a publicist or in marketing or something."

"I am. Managing to," she replies, rubbing her tiny belly. "I don't want to be aimless, although I guess I'll scale things back a bit when this baby comes along…"

"Hello, girls."

Axel appears behind us, clearly intending to spook me. And he does. I nearly jump.

"Axel!"

I wrap my arms around him and he tightly squeezes me back. My brother hasn't changed at all since the last time I saw him. He's tall, imposing, and trying to look uber slick and cool. His wavy black hair is shaped into his famous quiff and he's got those bright Stoll green eyes that I share. He truly hasn't changed from his teenage days.

"Of course Maddie is still working," he says. "She's working for Ravaged now. No way she wouldn't work; she's got that fiery determination that I fell in love with."

Maddie blushes again.

"Congratulations on the pregnancy, Axel," I say. "I can't believe I'm going to be an aunt."

"I can't believe you actually came to LA," he replies. "I thought you hated the place."

"Yeah, but what the hell? I want to see my brother."

"Don't you dare start getting affectionate," Axel sneers.

I turn to Maddie. "You two do know that I'm going to absolutely spoil the baby when it comes, right? You can't stop me."

"Was that your guitar I saw you carrying?" Maddie asks me.

Axel laughs. "Don't tell me it's the same one you've had since you first started to learn, Chloe. You didn't bring that all the way here, did you?"

"Yep," I reply, nudging my brother in the ribs for that comment. "It's special to me. That guitar has been my best friend for a decade. It's more reliable than any man has ever been."

"So you're as obsessed with music as much as your brother?" Maddie asks.

I snort. "More so."

Axel raises an eyebrow. "Really? You wanna bet on that?"

"I could outplay you on any instrument," I retort to my sibling. "Try me."

Maddie grabs my arm. "I'm so sorry. I haven't even asked you if you want something to drink. You must need a glass of wine after your flight. Come, get relaxed. Welcome."

I laugh. "I am pretty thirsty."

"Red or white?"

"White, please."

Maddie pours me a glass and gets Axel a cold beer. She pours herself a glass of sparkling water.

"I guess the worst thing about pregnancy is the fact you can't even have a drink to help you through it," I remark.

Maddie nods. "At least I can still make choc chip cookies. I love to do that when stressed."

"Oh God, I love those damn cookies," Axel says. "They're better than sex, trust me."

Maddie gives him a playful slap on the shoulder and turns back to me. "Here, have one."

Maddie passes me a freshly baked cookie. I bite into it and... *oh my God*, the flavor is amazing.

"This is amazing," I comment. "Orgasmic."

"Ah, so I see you have an equally foul mouth as your brother then," Maddie comments. "It's not just the green eyes you two share."

I take a seat on one of the bar stools in their large kitchen. Maddie's looking at Axel. He walks over to her and tucks away a strand of her hair behind her ear. They look so sweet together.

"It's good to see my brother in love," I say.

Maddie puts down her glass on the counter. "Have you got someone?" she asks. "A boy back in Crystal River?"

"Don't ask her that, Maddie," Axel interrupts.

"Oh, you don't have to answer, Chloe," Maddie quickly adds apologetically in her shy way. "I don't mean to pry."

"It's fine," I reply. "I haven't had anyone for quite some time. I'm too busy working."

"I can pay for your flight over here," Axel says. "Seeing as I invited you to come see us."

"No, it's okay."

"I know you don't have much, Chloe. I'm a freaking rockstar, I have spare change everywhere."

I purse my lips. I hate talking about the subject of money. Despite our shared green eyes and dirty mouths, Axel and I have very differing views on wealth. "I can pay for myself, thanks."

He's tried to offer me money before. Kickbacks from his music career. I've refused every time. I don't want to accept charity from my own brother, however stubborn that may seem.

Maddie senses the awkwardness and immediately buts in. "I saw that you've gone viral, Chloe. Astrid showed me."

"I didn't know that," Axel says. "Viral for what?"

"Just me singing one of my songs back home," I reply. "It's completely unexpected."

"She's being humble," Maddie says to her boyfriend. "She's got millions of views on it. You can't escape her face and her voice on social media right now. It's going stratospheric."

"I'm trying to avoid looking at the comments underneath the video," I say.

"Oh, there's bound to be some shitty ones," Maddie says. "But you really just got millions of views *in a freaking day*. You should be proud of yourself and your work. You're an overnight success, Chloe. You've got to be feeling over the moon about that."

"An overnight success of ten years pumping out music," I reply with a slight smile. It really has been years of work to even get a video to go viral. Years of me playing to practically no one in my bedroom. "But, yeah, it's pretty damn cool."

I haven't told either of them my other reason for coming to LA. The meeting with Mickey Miller. I just want to keep that quiet. Maybe it's because I'm freaking the hell out over it. My God, the nerves I have. My hands were practically shaking on the plane. The person in the seat next to me must've thought I have a phobia of flying.

"Working hard for years with no immediate reward is how things are done," Axel says.

I scoff. "It was easy for you. You boys jumped out of the gate into stardom. Girls usually have to work a lot harder."

"Look, if I can give you some unsolicited advice, Chloe,"

Maddie says. "As a publicist, please don't check the numbers and comments on the video. The internet can really be a cruel place."

"I agree," Axel says. "I made the mistake on Ravaged's first album and... *wow*. Those comments. Even *I* was rattled."

"I've already been getting lots of messages and comments from Tainted Lives fans," I say. That band is Ravaged's rival, as if their fans didn't tell me enough times. "They're ruthless, those guys. Simply because I'm your sister, Axel."

"Tainted Lives don't do anything to discourage their rabid fanbase," my brother says with a sigh. "In fact, they encourage them. That's why I hate that fucking band."

"They're not so bad," Maddie remarks.

"You did get on the receiving end of one of their stupid pranks," Axel comments.

"Well, yeah," Maddie says, turning to me. "We met Tainted Lives at the airport and they thought it would be hilarious to squirt me down with water from a hose. It was a *lot* of fun. Not."

"Wow."

"Ugh. I don't want to talk about them," Axel says. "The assholes."

"So, with your baby," I jump in, changing the subject. "Are you going to raise them in this house? It's a lovely home."

Maddie smiles. "That's the plan. We like it here. It's easy for both of us, especially with Axel touring."

"I think you and I are going to be good friends," I say to her.

"I think so too."

From the open front door comes a stranger's voice. "Axel? Maddie? I'm here to pick up that guitar I lent you."

We all look up towards the hallway leading to the front.

Wait.

That isn't a stranger's voice.

I recognize that man's deep baritone any day, even though it's been years.

*Fuck. Fuckity fuck.*

I thought I would be able to avoid him on this trip to LA, but who was I kidding? I should not have been naïve to think that I wouldn't run into the man who broke my heart while here. The same man responsible for me being stuck behind a till on minimum wage in my hometown for seven years.

I glance around me. There's no way out of this house. No way without looking like a total jackass in front of my brother's girlfriend.

And, besides, it's too late. He's already here.

The man strolls into Axel and Maddie's kitchen like he owns the place, and he immediately locks eyes with me.

*Fuck.*

Yep. It's him. The man who took my virginity.

Bishop Hayes.

# 3

*CHLOE*

THERE's complete silence as Bishop Hayes walks into Maddie and Axel's kitchen and locks eyes with me. It feels like it lasts for an eternity before the guitarist for Ravaged speaks.

"Well, this is a surprise," he mutters, unfazed. "Chloe Stoll. In the flesh. I didn't expect to find you here."

Like my brother, he has not changed. Not in seven years. It's been hard not to see him around the place all this time, what with his face being on billboards and posters and TV and Instagram as part of Ravaged, but even then I must admit that it feels like all the years have washed away the minute I see him in person and we're suddenly transported back to being two innocent teenagers about to make love for the first time. All those emotions I've kept buried away suddenly rise up in me like a burst dam...

The gentle way he once kissed me.

The confident way he made me feel so safe when we were together.

The thrill of him sneaking into my bedroom at night simply to touch me.

How he's whispered that I was a good girl. *His* good girl.

*Goddamn it.*

It's never been a wonder why Bishop is one of the biggest stars on the planet. I mean, just look at the guy. He's so gosh-darn-it handsome.

Tall. Sharp. Cheekbones to die for. Cute dimples. Deep brown eyes. An athletic, toned body sprayed with tattoos. Cutting eyes under his slicked back dark brown tousle of hair.

*Fuckity fuck.*

But then I remember the bad times. The memories of what he did to me.

And I am lost for words.

Everyone in the kitchen is all waiting for my reply – Maddie, Axel, and Bishop himself - and I have absolutely nothing to say.

It's up to Maddie to break the awkward silence.

"You guys know each other?" she asks.

Bishop smiles at her question. Axel looks away.

*Oh, he knows.*

Maddie clearly has no clue what's gone on between the man standing in her kitchen and her boyfriend's sister. I'm guessing Axel hasn't told her what happened.

"Yep," Bishops replies. "We know each other for sure."

Maddie shrugs, not grasping the extent of the issue at hand. "I guess you would, being Axel's best friend."

"Well, it's been a few years since Chloe and I have actually seen each other..."

"Seven years," I reply curtly. "*Seven.*"

"Hm." Oh, Bishop is such a tormentor. "Seven years is a long time, isn't it, Chloe?"

"Yep."

Maddie's gaze swivels between the two of us.

"Chloe and I used to be very close," Bishop explains to Maddie. *Close?* God, he's so infuriating. He knows he's winding me up by being so... casual. "I wonder why we aren't anymore, though."

"I've got nothing to say to you, Bishop," I say.

*I've got to nip this early in the bud. I can't be having this conversation.*

Let's just say that seeing Bishop again was not why I came to this city.

"Things are clearly awkward, and I was just here for my guitar," Bishop says, raising his hands in mock surrender. "I don't mean to start a riot or anything."

"The guitar's in the hallway," Axel says flatly, still not making any sort of eye contact with the rest of us. He clearly doesn't want to be drawn into this. It's as awkward for my brother as it is for me.

"Ah, great," Bishop replies. "I'll get it on my way out. I'm sure I'll see you around, Chloe. Goodbye, everyone."

"Bye," Maddie says. She glances at me with a curious expression. She now senses something's up, but she really has no idea how deep this all goes.

*Great.*

But before he heads down the hallway, Bishop spins around.

"Congratulations on going viral, Chloe," he says. "I always knew you were good. Really fucking good."

That hits me.

"Are you joking or being serious?" I ask him sharply.

"Oh, I'm being serious." His face is unreadable. He could be taking me for a ride with those fancy words. The man certainly comprehends how effective his words are at stinging me. Hell, even with all these years apart, he still understands me better than anyone else on planet Earth.

He knows all the ways to make me hurt. "You shouldn't check any comments on your video, though. There are some crazy people out there."

"Thanks for the completely unasked-for advice," I retort, crossing my arms and staring him down.

Bishop ignores me and looks over my shoulder at Maddie's choc chip cookies. He nonchalantly strolls back and helps himself to one in front of the rest of us.

Silence.

I don't take my eyes off him as he crunches into the cookie and closes his eyes for dramatic effect.

"*Orgasmic*," he says, breaking the quiet. He then turns to me. "You should try one of these, Chloe. It might loosen you up."

And then he goes.

We sit there in utter silence as his footsteps echo down the hallway.

It's only when we hear him close the front door that I realize I've been holding my breath the entire time.

# 4

*CHLOE*

I CAN HEAR BISHOP HAYES' heartbeat. My hand moves across his chest as my head rests literally an inch away from his beating organ.

*Thud. Thud. Thud.*

"Satisfied, Chloe?" Bishop asks me in a whisper. "Can you hear it?"

"Yes," I say as I slowly raise my head to face Bishop. He's smiling at me. That goddamn beautiful smile that makes me giddy inside. "I can hear you."

"It's weird that we've got all this... biology happening inside us," he replies, taking my hand that's tracing over his bare muscular chest. "To be honest, it freaks me out a bit."

"Hey, that's a good idea for a song."

"What?"

"You know, talking about how we've got all these organs in us, but what we're really guided by is our hearts."

"Damn, Chloe. You're pretty good at this songwriting thing."

I don't know how joking he's being, but his words make my own heart melt.

I lower my head against his chest again so that I can once more hear his heartbeat.

*Thud. Thud. Thud.*

The rest of my body is draped over Bishop. We're both naked. Basking in that post-sex glow.

Being with Bishop feels right, more right than anything else. I had thought, when he started sneaking through my bedroom window, that I might begin to doubt everything that's gone on between us, and yet there hasn't been one glimmer of this not feeling just *right*.

"I never expected us to end up together," I say to Bishop. "Not when we first met."

The eighteen-year-old snorts. "What? When we were, like, ten?"

I giggle. "Um, yeah."

"Well I, for one, have always known I'd end up with you, Chloe. I fancied you the first time I saw you."

"Come on, Bishop, don't mock..."

"It's true. Sometimes guys just know when they see the girl that will be their everything, the girl that every other girl in their life will be held up against. The girl who every other girl will never compare to. You're *that* girl, Chloe, for me. For real."

I don't know how to react to that other than to pinch him. He doesn't even react to the pain except to laugh.

"You're a real sweetheart, Bishop. *You* should be a song-writer with the honey that you can speak."

"Don't call me sweetheart."

"You might've been thinking all that, but me, at ten years old, wasn't really thinking which of my brother's friends I would fuck one day."

"You were being pretty narrow-minded, then."

"Ha, ha. Very funny."

Bishop squeezes my hand. "I spoke to Drake Sharpe today," he says softly, as if broaching something dark and serious.

"Oh, yeah?"

I know Drake Sharpe. Not well, though. He's a friend of my brother's. He and Bishop are only close in that they attend the same year at Crystal River High and that they have mutual friends in common. Bishop telling me he spoke to Drake is unusual, but not abnormal or anything. I wonder why he's bringing him up.

"He's pretty intent on forming a band at high school this year," Bishop continues. "He's spoken to the teachers and everything and is looking to organize something. He told me he's going to hold auditions in the gym, hopefully soon."

I nod

"Yeah, Axel told me something like that, but he didn't mention Drake. He told me he's considering doing it, and now I guess he'll be a shoo-in, of course, being a friend of Drake's."

"And also for being fucking awesome at the bass," Bishop adds.

"Yeah. He's been practicing like he's possessed."

"He hasn't told me he was thinking about doing it, though," Bishops says. "Why not?"

I shake my head. "I think he thinks it's silly. He's worried that if all this goes nowhere, then it's embarrassing. He spends all his spare time in his room now, though, rehearsing like mad."

"Like I said, Axel is fucking talented," Bishop remarks. "I bet he'll be going places."

I nod.

"I hate to admit it, but it's true."

"Music runs in your family's blood," Bishop says.

I blush. "Maybe..."

"Why don't you think about auditioning for Drake's band?"

"What?"

I narrow my eyes.

"You'll be a shoo-in too, you know," Bishop reasons. "Axel's talented sister. You'll both be great in a band together. Isn't that what you said you wanted to do?"

"I'm too shy to ever even *think* about auditioning, Bishop. You know me."

"Come on, I've heard you sing and play."

"Yeah, only in the safety and security of this bedroom," I retort with a sigh. "I'm insecure, okay? I can't perform in front of other people."

"You do know it's a requisite of being a rockstar to play in front of an audience, right? You can't really tour the world not being able to go on a stage, Chloe."

I take in a long breath. "I'm scared."

"Yeah, and you push through it. That's what being a performer means. Have you not watched a single documentary about bands? Everyone's scared of going in front of others when they start out."

"My... scaredness is more than other people's, Bishop. It's ingrained in me. I'm worried that people will laugh. Axel is the extroverted one of the two of us. He's the one people gravitate to. I'm just the younger sister who fades into the background."

"Audition, Chloe," Bishops says seriously. No hint of his jokiness at all. "Trust me, you're good."

"You're telling me to really audition for Drake's band?"

Bishop nods.

"Yeah, I can help you if you're feeling under-confident. I do know how to play the guitar, you know."

I scoff. "I'm better than you, though."

Bishop sits up, forcing me to sit up as well. He stares me deep in the eyes. "Be serious. You should audition. I know it's the right thing for you."

I shrug. "Maybe you should audition instead of me. You would be good at it."

"I won't. I don't care much for music. But you should, you should be in a band, Chloe. You should be a rockstar, not me."

I fall back against the softness of my bed with a long sigh. "I'll think about it."

Bishop leans down and wraps an arm around me. He holds me tight.

My finger absentmindedly traces around the long faint scar on his chest.

"How did you get this?" I ask him quietly. "This scar? I've always seen it and always wondered how it happened."

"I got it when I was a kid. Before I met you."

"How?"

"I was being an idiot. I was chasing some bully from school and we ran into a farm. I got myself caught up in barbed wire. This is the proof that you really shouldn't do that."

"Ouch."

"But I still managed to get that bully in the end, even though I was profusely bleeding. He deserved that beating."

"You're pretty relentless, Bishop."

"One thing you must know about me, Chloe, is that I'm competitive. When I get my mind fixated on something, I don't stop until I've got it. I'll move hell or high water for what I want."

"Well, you've got me."

"I know."

There's another long pause until I decide to speak again.

"Something has been weighing on my mind, Bishop."

"What is it?"

*Here goes.*

"I want to talk to my brother about us."

Bishop doesn't say anything at first as my words soak in.

And then he says my name. Like he's trying to stop my thoughts.

"*Chloe...*"

"We can't continue sneaking around like this forever, Bishop."

"I think we can," he replies.

"You know it would be worse if Axel were to walk in on us, here, in my bed together. It's only a matter of time before something crazy like that were to happen."

"I don't know about that," Bishop says.

"We can break it to him softly. In a manner of our own choosing..."

"Axel would go crazy if he found out," Bishop continues. "He would try to kill me, Chloe. You don't usually let one of your best friends fuck your younger sister, do you? How do you think you would react if you were as proud and as impulsive as your brother?"

My finger reaches the bottom of his chest scar. He got this pursuing something he wanted. I wonder how many scars he might get from pursuing me.

I have no answer for him.

# 5

*CHLOE*

WHEN BISHOP LEAVES, both Maddie and Axel pretend to act like nothing's happened, which I'm eternally grateful for. I don't want to talk about Ravaged's guitarist. I don't even want to be reminded that he was just here, in freaking front of me, just moments ago.

And I certainly don't want to talk about Bishop with my brother, of all people.

"I'll show you Chloe's viral video," Maddie says to my brother as she pulls out her phone.

I shake my head. "You don't have to do that, Maddie."

"Oh, I really want to see this," Axel smirks.

They both sit there and watch the entirety of my song.

"Switch it off," I protest, but they ignore me. I hate hearing myself back. I'm freaking out that they're judging me. They don't talk or comment at all during the video, and it's pure agony.

They don't even make a sound until the very end.

"You're *good*," Axel remarks as Maddie switches off her phone. "Really fucking good, Chloe."

"You don't have to please me."

"Shut up. You're fucking good. I've always told you that, but you've always hated performing for me, so I never see it. Your persistence for working hard all these years has paid off."

"Ugh." I hate taking compliments.

"So, tell me, why haven't you performed for me before?" he asks.

"Because I'm shy, Axel. I'm worried about choking up."

My brother narrows his eyes. "I don't understand."

"I just find performing in public something really hard to do," I reply.

Maddie turns to me. "Hey, Chloe, from one introvert to another, I understand."

"You girls," Axel moans.

"I think I'll have another glass of wine," I say. Axel pours me one, watching me. I know he's thinking about Bishop, but I also know he won't say anything about the man. We don't ever talk about Axel's best friend, or what went down between us all those years ago.

"So, what's the real reason you're here in Los Angeles?" Axel asks me. "You've told me multiple times you don't like the place and all the fakery here. Surely, you're not just here to see a not-very-visibly pregnant Maddie?"

"Hey, of course I want to see Maddie. You've hidden her from me. She's all Mom talks about at home."

"Thank you, Chloe," Maddie says.

"You've made quite an impression on Mom when she came to visit," I reply. "She really likes you."

"There must be something else, Chloe," Axel interrogates.

*Damn. He knows me too well.*

"Well, because of the viral video, I do have a meeting scheduled. They wanted me to fly out here pretty quick to meet them."

"A music producer wants to meet you?" Axel asks, his eyebrow raising. "Which one?"

"Yeah. Mickey Miller."

"Amazing!" Maddie claps her hands together.

Axel's face drops.

"He's Ravaged's producer," he whispers.

"I had a feeling he was," I reply.

"He's a scary dude, Chloe," my brother warns. "But he's the best in the business."

"Well, I have a meeting with him all booked. I think he might want me as a client."

"And all because of this video?" Maddie asks.

"Yep."

"Why don't you talk to this producer guy for Chloe?" Maddie questions her brother. "I'm sure a good word from you will help. He *does* represent you, after all."

"We don't see him much," Axel explains. "And, from his reputation, he's not one of those types who takes kindly to requests. He's not a fan of nepotism."

"I've always wanted to achieve things on my own anyway," I say. "Without the help of my brother being in one of the biggest bands on the planet."

"That's a noble trait," Maddie remarks, nodding.

"Trust me, Chloe," Axel tells me. "A single word from Mickey Miller can make or break someone's career."

Maddie elbows him in the side. "That's not very helpful, Axel."

"Ah, no pressure or anything," I reply. "*Everything* I've ever worked for hinges on this meeting. Got it."

I already knew all that, but hearing it from Axel doesn't help. Maybe I should turn around now and head back home. I'm only going to fail at any public performance in front of this record producer anyway. What the hell was I thinking coming here in the first place?

"You can stay here in our house," Axel suggests. "We've got plenty of space. And bedrooms."

"Yep, Chloe," Maddie says. "You're welcome to stay as long as you'll like."

"Thank you," I reply. "But like with Mickey Miller, I'll prefer to do things myself. I've booked a temporary place to stay on an app already."

"I get you," Maddie says, nodding again.

I check the time on my phone. "I actually have to start heading over there now."

"I can drive you," Axel says, rising from his stool.

"I'm okay, I'll get a taxi. Stay here and look after your lovely pregnant girlfriend."

"Hey, I've literally just tested positive. I'm not immobile."

"You sure?" Axel asks me.

"I want to do this all myself," I reply. "I hope you don't take that badly. I just don't want a repeat of what happened in high school."

Axel sits back down. "I understand."

I say goodbye to Maddie. I tell her we've got to meet up in the next few days, and she gives me good luck for the meeting. I collect my bags and head out the front door.

I order a taxi on my phone. The app says it's going to be ten minutes. I'm happy to wait outside the house. Just me. Alone.

*Okay, Los Angeles. Give me your best shot.*

I know this is going to be my one chance at success on my own terms. I better not screw up this meeting. As Axel reminded me in there, everything hinges on Mickey Miller's verdict. But I shouldn't worry because I've spent years getting ready for this moment.

But it's fair to say my nerves are freaking the *hell* out right now.

Suddenly, a car pulls up in front of me. Tinted windows. I can't see inside. It screeches.

This is no taxi.

*What the hell?*

The vehicle stops, and Bishop Hayes steps out of the side passenger seat. He looks straight at me with a fiery intensity. There's no doubt he's here because of me.

He speaks before I even have a chance to react.

"You and I need to talk, Chloe."

# 6

SEVEN YEARS AGO

*CHLOE*

ANOTHER NIGHT with Bishop in my bed. My room's window is still open from when he stealthily crawled in here not even an hour ago. A slight breeze wafts in so we lie under the bedsheets to keep ourselves warm.

And to be as close as possible to each other.

"Favorite color?" he asks, whispering so as to not alert Axel or my mom.

Bishop and I are playing a silly questions game. It's an easy way to find out the most random and irreverent trivia about each other. I was doubtful about its merits when he suggested it to me, but it's actually kinda fun.

"Green," I reply. "Try something harder."

"Okay. Favorite food?"

I roll my eyes. "That's easy. Seafood."

He looks at me with disgust. "You like seafood?"

"Come on, is that one of your questions?"

Bishop laughs. "No. Fine, then. Favorite sex position?"

I hit him playfully on the arm. "I'm not telling you that."

"Why not?"

"It's for you to find out. If you're lucky."

I feel his hard erection press against my leg. It helps that we're both naked. I'm not going to give him the satisfaction of playing with his member, though. He's gonna have to work a little harder to get me frisky.

"You're making things difficult, Chloe. Right, I'm going to shoot through some quick-fire ones. Sound good?"

"Shoot ahead."

"Indoors or outdoors?" he asks.

"Indoors."

"Favorite TV show?"

"Gilmore Girls."

"Favorite animal?"

"Super random, but I guess a snow leopard. They're very cute."

Bishop smiles. "If money didn't matter, what would you buy yourself?"

Oh. That question makes me think. He's really got me there.

But I do have an answer. Something I've actually never told anyone.

"A Gibson guitar, for sure. They're the best. Definitely an older model, something real classy. I've always wanted one, but they are super expensive."

Bishop nods at me. "That's nice. I guess most people will say some kind of stupid car."

"My brother would say that. He dreams of buying a motorbike."

"That's *so* Axel."

"And what about you?"

"I don't really give a shit about money," Bishop replies. "I'm more interested in the work."

"For being such a popular guy at school, you're really into your academia, aren't you? Breaking all the cliches."

Bishop shrugs. "I like to work hard. What's wrong with that? If I'm doing something, I might as well be my very best at it."

"I like that about you," I reply.

"And your focus is what I like about you," he says. "You really want to be a rockstar."

"I just want to play my guitar and sing," I reply bluntly.

"You really care about your music, don't you?"

"Yep. Did I win those quick-fire questions, then?"

Bishop smiles. His dimples kill me. "I think so."

I wink at him. "Does that mean you lose?"

"Oh," he says, his voice lowering to a sexy purr. "I *never* lose, Chloe."

He kisses me. I close my eyes and surrender myself to his warmth. I'm beginning to savor every kiss with this man.

He's strong, confident, and smart. Also damn funny. He makes me feel like the only woman in the world. What else could a girl want?

I feel like I've hit some kind of invisible jackpot.

*Knock, knock.*

Someone's at my door, and everything turns into panic.

"Chloe..."

It's Axel's voice on the other side.

"Axel? What is it?" I ask, concealing my sudden horror.

"Is everything okay? I can hear voices?"

I turn to Bishop and whisper sharply to him. "Get out."

"You don't need to say that twice," he replies soundlessly as he leaps out from my bed and through the open window.

46

"Maybe you should go see a doctor if you're hearing voices," I say to my brother.

"So funny, Chloe. I'm coming in."

*Typical Axel to barge in whenever he feels like it...*

The door opens, and I pray to whoever's listening that Bishop's escaped in time. Axel's eyes dart from the open window to me in my bed.

"What do you want, Axel?"

"You're in bed already?" he asks. By the look on his face, I think – I *hope* - he doesn't suspect a thing. Especially not his best friend having just been in here.

I hope. I hope. I hope.

"Yeah, what's wrong with getting some beauty sleep?"

He ignores all semblance of my privacy and sits down on the edge of my bed. "I want to show you a song I've been working hard at."

Before I can answer, he glances back at the window. His eyes narrow. I've lived with my stupid brother long enough to know that he's starting to think.

*Holy shit.*

Okay, maybe he's starting to piece the clues together...

"Um, can I hear the song?" I ask quickly, trying to divert his attention.

"Maybe I'll show you another day," Axel says, heading back to the door. "I'll leave you to get your... beauty sleep."

He shuts the door, and I breathe out a sigh of relief.

That was close. Too close. How long will Bishop and my luck last? It would be the worst thing if Axel finds us together rather than me just breaking the news softly to my brother, but that's not what Bishop wants. He's made that very clear.

*Damn.*

Danger was averted, but how long can we keep this up?

# 7

*CHLOE*

Even though Bishop tells me we need to talk, I don't say a single thing as I stand, waiting for the taxi, outside Maddie and Axel's house. I don't care about social etiquette; I want to twist the knife in. Make him feel awkward. I'm not going to submit to his demands simply because he's surprised me outside my brother's home.

He wants *us* to *talk*? Well, he can stick my words up his pompous ass.

I look behind him at the car he's so dramatically arrived in. He wasn't driving; he exited via the passenger seat.

*I know exactly what's going on.*

"Hello, Drake," I say to the tinted window, completely ignoring the man standing in front of me.

Bishop laughs. I still ignore him. "You were always super perceptive, weren't you, Chloe," he tells me.

I still ignore him as the car's tinted window rolls down. And there is Drake Sharpe. Frontman of Ravaged. Staring back at me with his shit-eating grin.

"Hello, Chloe," he says in his smooth lead-singer voice. "Still looking as gorgeous as ever."

"Your playboy ways might work with your throwaway groupies, but they ain't gonna work with me, Drake. I remember when you were a teenage boy and couldn't hold down a single beer without throwing up on my mother's driveway."

"Ouch. You're not only still gorgeous, but you're still a biter, Chloe."

Like Bishop, the lead singer of Ravaged hasn't changed from when we were kids in the same class at high school. He's always been so incredibly and infuriatingly good looking. Thick, glossy hair, with a delicious curl that dangles over his brow. Blue angelic eyes. Perfect skin. Just the hint of stubble. A real hit with the ladies, and he knows it. Drake Sharpe is cocky and arrogant and amazing with his words. He's tall and rough and gives off those bad boy vibes that make him both dangerous and irresistible at the same time. A charismatic show-off, he's a rough diamond with spikes that can hurt you. It'll take a real woman to tame his feral side. I don't doubt that. The rockstar does what he likes, when he likes, and he really doesn't give a shit about what others think of him, and yet he's extremely loyal to the few people that are important in his life. Plus, he's hot, famous, talented, and unbelievably rich. No wonder every girl that meets him simply swoons. I, on the other hand, have always just seen him as a friend. It was Bishop I had eyes for when we were teenagers. But, hey, I can appreciate a handsome man, especially if that'll make Bishop deservedly jealous.

"How's life going for you, Drake?" I ask him with a smirk. "Found a girl yet that you're gonna settle down with?"

"You know me, Chloe. No girls. That's my one rule."

"That one rule still going strong?"

49

"I'm still a free man, so yeah."

"One day you're going to find that girl and love is going to hit you like a ton of bricks, trust me," I tell him.

"That day will never come, Chloe."

Bishop wryly glances between us two, clearly a little bit frustrated not to get in a word. I want him to wait for my attention. He doesn't even deserve it. I'm going to talk to Drake as long as I want.

And I know Drake is enjoying making his friend and fellow band member wait as well. It's refreshing to make the serious tallest member of Ravaged uncomfortable for once in his confident life.

"I've heard Ravaged is doing quite well," I remark.

"Yep, quite well indeed. Our new album has been number one for months. We're smashing the records."

"Good for you. It's what you always wanted. Are Ravaged still intending to perform at Madison Square Garden one day as you've always said?"

Drake nods.

"That's been our dream."

"Good luck."

"Thanks."

I've not forgotten about Bishop all this time. I've really been twisting in the knife, ignoring him completely.

"And how about you, Bishop?" I ask the man dryly, finally turning to him. "Were you just waiting for me to step out of my brother's place to ambush me?"

"Yes."

He's unfazed by my directness. It's annoying, but kind of hot.

Drake begins to wind up his tinted window. "I'll give you two a bit of privacy," he says.

I stare at Bishop. "What would you do if I decided to just walk back into Axel's house right now?" I ask him.

"I'd do nothing."

"You seem keen to talk to me. Would you follow me inside?"

"You want me to be all manly, rip open my shirt, and break down the door to carry you back to my cave to tie you up until you want to be mine?"

"No..."

"You're blushing, Chloe. Did I get you there?"

"I'm pissed off and just want my cab to arrive." I take out my phone to check the app. Seven minutes away.

*Seven more minutes with Bishop.*

"Let's cut the bullshit," the rockstar says with a growl. "I want to sleep with you, Chloe."

"Wow," I reply, shocked. "There's that famous dirty mouth of yours. Has being a famous musician made you forget all levels of general politeness?"

"Hey, what can I say? I find you very attractive, Chloe. I like to get what I want."

"Gross."

"I say what I want, and I usually get it."

"And I'm guessing you want me?"

"Exactly."

"Maybe this might be one of the times you, unfortunately, don't get what you want."

"I want you to want me, Chloe. It's going to happen."

"Just saying that doesn't erase the past, or what went down between us."

"It *has* been a long time," Bishop says. "Aren't you over your hatred of me?"

"It isn't pretty when two hearts break, Bishop."

"I see. So you haven't changed then?"

"Mom likes to say I've become a lot more cynical. Especially of pretty boys with honeyed words."

"I've noticed."

"Well, I guess it's time for you to go into Drake's car, then," I say, trying my best to hold firm. "We've got nothing to talk about."

But Bishop is not over with me yet.

"Have you got a boy waiting for you back in Crystal River?" he asks. "A boyfriend? Husband?"

"Wouldn't you like to know?"

He smiles. "So that's a *no*, then. Good. Perfect for me."

"Lay off it, Bishop. I'm never giving in to you or your demands."

"I'm going to be persistent, just like you."

"Yeah?"

"Chloe, it's time to drop the façade. I know you're still that girl whose window I used to sneak through."

"That girl is long gone," I reply sternly, holding my head high. "I'm not in Los Angeles for you. I would very much like for you to disappear off the face of the earth."

"That's a real shame," he replies. He takes a step towards me, penetrating into my personal space. I don't budge an inch, but I do ready myself. He's so big and broad-shouldered and just an intense presence. "Don't you remember the way we were both addicted to each other? How we couldn't get enough of each other's bodies? That we couldn't face time apart from each other?"

"Hm."

I'm stoic and unmoved. I also remember the hard times. How things ended.

But Bishop takes another step towards me, and I feel my defenses crumbling under his gaze.

He's a hard worker, that's for sure. He *really* doesn't like to lose.

However much I despise this man for what he did to me, he's still the only man I can talk to like this. Openly. Honestly. Even though we are at loggerheads right now, he's still *listening* to every word I say. No man has ever come close to this. He's paying complete attention to my body language and the way I'm speaking. His desire for me is clear as day.

*Who doesn't want to be wanted?* Even me, even with my stone-cold heart.

He's still making me feel, seven years later, like I'm the only woman in the world.

"I worshipped the ground beneath your feet," the rockstar says softly. "So how come we ever split apart? What have these last seven years been?"

"It was your fault," I whisper back at him.

"I remember the way you made me feel, Chloe. I remember the taste of your lips on mine. I want that again."

I say nothing as his hand moves to my face. He takes my cheek.

I don't move.

"What are you doing, Bishop?" My words are strong, but they come out of my mouth breathless and insincere. I know exactly what he's doing, and there's a part of me that doesn't want him to stop.

"Maybe we can start over again," Bishop says, his voice barely above a murmur.

I feel heat rise in me. My heart rate quickens.

He moves in his head. His lips are about to meet mine.

And then I take a step back.

His arm drops from my cheek.

"You betrayed me," I reply with a tilt up of my chin to face him. "Do you forget that?"

Bishop shrugs, but he knows the magic of the past minute has completely evaporated.

"We were both teenage idiots," he explains. "Maybe the past should be left in the past; you clearly still have feelings for me."

I shake my head. "Get lost, Bishop. The past is still important and I will never forget it."

"The past is the past."

"You're really not giving up, aren't you?" I accuse him. "You really do see everything as a competition to win."

"I never lose," Bishop replies. "I lost once. I lost the most important thing in my life."

"Which was what, exactly?"

Bishop doesn't even blink. "You."

I take in a sharp breath.

"You were my best friend," I say matter-of-factly. I don't want his words, however piercing they may be, to visibly affect me.

Bishop takes a moment to study my reaction. I try to remain stony-faced.

"I know," he eventually replies.

"In fact, you were more than my best friend," I clarify. "You were my *everything*."

"People can change, Chloe. I can change. Have you even thought of that?"

"You changing doesn't change what happened."

"You're not still hung up on all of *that*, surely?" he asks me. "It was nothing."

"It wasn't nothing."

"If anything, you should be angry at Axel. He was involved."

"I was. For a long time. But family is family. We mend and we fix things up."

"So I mean nothing to you? Nothing at all?"

"Yes."

Bishop sneers.

*He doesn't believe me.*

"That hurts, Chloe, but it's not true. I know it's not."

"I just want to get my taxi, Bishop. Get out of my way. Let me wait in peace."

"But this is the conversation we should've had seven years ago."

"It's way too late to have a conversation, Bishop, about anything."

"How about a kiss, then? Surely, that will change your mind. I know you still want me." I shake my head at his outrageous comment. "Give me another chance, Chloe."

*Never.*

Not even if he's professing his desire like this.

"You always had a flair for the dramatic, Bishop," I retort. "I've seen this story play out a million times before. Just because we once had a history doesn't mean you can simply slip back into my life."

There's a moment of silence between us. I look around at the dark LA streets, trying my best to avoid eye contact with this man who won't just... let go.

*He doesn't want to admit defeat. Typical Bishop.*

"You are still living in Crystal River?" he asks me.

I scrunch up my face at him, dreading what he means. "What's wrong with that?"

"Oh, nothing," Bishop replies. "How is that town? It's been a long time since I was last home."

"Things don't change back home. People still remember the ones who were asswipes, even if they've gone on to become world famous musicians."

"Don't forget incredibly rich."

"No, how could I forget that?"

"Are you in Los Angeles because of your viral video?" he asks me.

"Mind your own business."

"I saw it," he says softly. "I liked it."

"Good for you."

Bishop smirks again. "You know that I'll do anything to change your mind. Anything you want to do in bed."

The app pings me to say the taxi is reaching this street. I pick up my guitar and wheel my luggage close to me, ready.

"Don't beg, Bishop," I say. "It's not becoming of you."

"I know what I want, and I'm going to get it, Chloe. It's only a matter of time. You can feel the sparks between us just as I do."

"You're just gonna have to rely on your fantasies to do that job for you," I say. "My cab is here, and I'm going to go."

I brush past the man towards the taxi, waving to Drake through his tinted window as I walk by.

"Chloe..."

Bishop's going to try and stop me, I know.

But I interrupt him before he gets the chance.

"Goodbye forever, Bishop. I really hope I never see you again. See? You lose this time."

I get into the taxi and shut the door. We pull away.

I fall into the temptation of swiveling in my seat to look behind me. Bishop is just standing there on the curb, watching me leave with a blank expression.

He's never going to give up.

After all these years, that man can still wound me with a single look.

8

*CHLOE*

THE CAB DROPS me off at a car rental place, just where I need to go. Even I'm not dumb enough to know that you need a car to get around Los Angeles. It's another reason why I don't take a liking to this city. Everything's just so spread out like it's purposely designed to make you feel like nothing but a tiny ant. Meaningless. Ready to be chewed up and spat out by any one of the massive entertainment industry factories here. It makes LA one hell of a scary place, that's for sure.

I hand over my practically last dollars to hire a car. It burns me up to sign the forms at the rental place.

*This is it. Risking everything for this viral video.*

Make or break.

I'm old and mature enough to wise up to the fact that sometimes in life you only get one opportunity at cracking something, and this is mine. This upcoming meeting with Mickey Miller *is* that opportunity.

The woman behind the desk hands me the keys to the

rental and I try not to let my fingers shake with nerves as I take them from her.

* * *

"HOLY SHIT, I KNOW YOU."

It's the immediate reaction I get when the door to the apartment I'm renting opens.

"Um, hi."

"Where do I know you from? Where? Wait, don't tell me. Let me think... Oh, *right*. Holy shit. That song, yeah? The one everyone's *obsessed* with that's doing the rounds on Instagram? That's you. Yep. Definitely you. Hello!"

Standing before me is a very large man, I'm guessing probably in his early thirties, who has the bushiest beard this side of a ye olde pirate ship. His expressive voice loudly echoes out into the hallway like a trained opera singer. In the single minute I've spent with him, I can already tell he's bombastic, super friendly, and *incredibly* flamboyant.

A guy that makes me instantly laugh.

"Yep. I'm Chloe Stoll. I'm the girl from that song. Gosh, that's weird saying that."

"Gary Seal, at your service," my host replies with a theatrical bow. "Web designer and rental host by day, raging queer by night."

"I guess this is the right address, then," I say.

"Let me tell you, I did not know that a freaking starlet was staying at my place," Gary says. "I would've actually cleaned it properly if I knew it was you coming. I absolutely *adore* your voice, Chloe. I'm going to have to make you sing for me before you leave. It's now part of your rental contract."

I giggle again. "Please, don't."

He's warmed me up after that insane experience with

Bishop. It's nice to meet someone so gregarious and extroverted as Gary, especially in such a cutthroat city as Los Angeles. I'm already happy with my choice of rental apartment if he's the owner.

"Come in," he says. "Don't be shy. Welcome to my little abode here in the City of Angels. I'll show you around. Come on, come on. In you pop."

Gary practically pulls me inside. It's a very neat place. The wall is full of hanging framed photos of Gary with friends and family. The man must have a buzzing social life and it's pretty evident why. He's like a whirlwind of fun.

"I don't know what you're saying about not being clean, Gary," I exclaim. "Your place is spotless. There's no need to scrub down anything. I wish my place back home was like this."

"Thank you. You can stay, Chloe Stoll."

"I think I will."

"Tell me, whereabouts are you from? You're too nice to be from this town."

"A small town on the other side of the country."

"Ah. A small town girl in the big city with a gay roommate. It's like the start of a sitcom. I love it. Is that your guitar?"

I nod as I take off the guitar case from off my back. "Yep."

"I love that. God damn, you're so freaking talented. What's it like becoming internet famous?"

"Pretty crazy, if I'm honest. I wouldn't call myself famous."

"I've heard about you, so that certainly counts for something."

"I guess so," I reply.

"What are you doing in Los Angeles, then? Why aren't

you back home celebrating and getting drunk and having an orgy?" he asks me.

"Well, I'm making my dreams a reality, thanks to the boost coming from the video."

"You go, girl. That's what I love to hear."

I blush. "Thanks, Gary."

"You can have my room. I call it my dungeon. It's bigger than my spare room."

His room is no dungeon at all.

"I can't take your room, Gary. It's too nice, and I'm your guest. You can't sleep in the spare room."

"I insist. There are only a few times in life when some talented person who's about to launch into the stratosphere stays at your place. I want you to feel welcome in my city and take all that stress out of your life. I want to facilitate your stardom, and then I'll be able to ride on the coattails of your success for many years, Chloe. It's purely selfish on my part."

I giggle. "Right."

"I want to say on dates as your songs play in the background of the bar that *I knew that girl. She stayed in my bedroom, not merely my spare room but in my actual bed.*"

"You're funny, Gary."

"Darling, you haven't even properly met me yet. What are you doing tonight?"

I shrug. "I dunno. Maybe some practice. Unpack. Unwind."

Gary points a finger at me. "No way. A girl like you who's just gotten her first whiff of internet success? I'm going to take you out tonight. I'm going to get you drunk."

# 9

*BISHOP*

DRAKE DOESN'T SAY a thing to me until we're a twenty minutes drive away from Axel and Maddie's. It's only then, when infuriated by his silence, that I finally bite the bone and bark at my friend and bandmate.

"What is it?"

Drake just smiles at my outburst and puts his foot down on the gas, speeding his Ferrari along the winding highway.

"Nothing."

I can't contain another outburst.

"Don't you dare smirk at me, asshole."

"It was funny watching you with Chloe," he says calmly, infuriating me even more. "You really tried all your moves on her, didn't you? And yet, none of them worked. Hilarious."

"Oh, I'm not afraid of beating your ass," I retort with a huff. "Even if you are driving."

Drake chuckles and I mumble obscenities under my breath and try to focus on the LA scenery zooming past us.

I didn't plan on seeing Chloe today. Not at all. But seeing her was a welcome surprise. I haven't forgotten her at all these past seven years. She looks like the same girl I once fell in love with. Those green eyes, the same as her family's. Her long black hair. Just as she was in my dreams. Seeing her again today has stirred feelings inside me that I thought were long repressed.

*I've been waiting*
*every day of my life for you*
*Waiting for time to bring us together*
*Now that you're mine, I can't believe*
*That this is forever*

I'VE NEVER FORGOTTEN those lyrics she wrote about me. For me.

All those years... I've still thought about her like it was yesterday. Taking her virginity. Falling for someone for the first time. The hardest I've ever fallen.

*Fuck me*, the way she acted outside her brother's house. How close I got to stealing another kiss from her after all this time. She was leaning into it, I could tell. She was pushing me away with her words, but her body was betraying her feelings.

*God damnit*.

She still knows exactly how to make my head, and my heart, spin like a tumble dryer.

No girl can even compete. Will *ever* compete.

"What are you planning to do about Miss Chloe Stoll?" Drake asks me. "I mean, you're clearly still totally enamored with her. That much is fucking obvious."

I sigh. If there's anyone on this planet that can guess how I'm feeling, it's my stupid bandmates. We're closer than brothers in Ravaged. I can huff and puff all I like, but there's no hiding the truth from the men I share my life with.

"She's gorgeous. She's beautiful..."

"Don't let Axel hear you saying those words. He'll beat you to a pulp."

Ah. Axel. Another issue standing in the way. Man, the Stoll family is one prickly bunch to deal with. It makes things difficult that I love both of them. In different ways.

"Why did I ever let her go?" I ponder out loud. "Why did I lose her?"

I never speak about Chloe or about what happened to anyone, but her arriving here today has flipped the whole earth on its head. That's why I got Drake to spin the car around and take me back to Axel's place. I knew – *hoped* -

I'd catch Chloe leaving at some point, and I couldn't trust myself to drive in the state I was. Seeing her again up close like that reduced me to being a nervous in-love teenage boy all over again. Even if he *is* an annoying brat, I wanted Drake right beside me when I ambushed the girl.

"Yeah," Drake adds. "I don't know why you would let her go when she's such a good piece of ass."

I raise my fist towards Ravaged's lead singer.

"You want me to fuck you up, Drake? Show her some respect. She's Axel's sister."

"Should I treat her with the same respect as you treated her back in high school?"

I shake my head. "Why is everyone on my fucking ass tonight? Is it *shit-on-Bishop* day?"

"I mean, you did do a pretty shitty thing to her," Drake says with a shrug.

I growl. "I know."

"So you can see why she might be a *little* wary of you, huh?"

"Do you think she still likes me?" I ask my friend.

*What the hell have I turned into? A lovesick puppy?*

"Hey, she didn't run away at the first sight of you, so that's good news, isn't it? You might have to grovel and beg to even get her attention, but at least she heard you out."

"I don't grovel or beg," I snarl back.

Drake just laughs. "Well, you've got to do some kind of pleading after the way you treated her."

"You were the one who didn't let her join Ravaged."

"But I wasn't the guy who broke her heart."

"Drake..."

"First, it's Axel with Maddie, and now it's you with Chloe. Remember those rules we made as a band? The music is what's important, not the girls."

"I know."

"I won't have this band's quality sacrificed because you and Axel's dicks fall in love," Drake says sternly.

"Man, you're being rude tonight."

"Remember those rules, Bishop. Ravaged is the most important thing in our lives. The band will suffer if you guys all start focusing on girls instead of what we've got here."

*Drake and these rules. They were fine when we were teenagers, just starting out as a band, but now...*

"I wouldn't lose sight of our mission, Drake. Even if Chloe's back in town."

"Good to hear."

"Let's just leave it at that." I don't want a fight. I know how unmovable Drake is on this topic.

"Yep. Just remember what the most important thing is."

Breaking up our little tit-for-tat is Drake's phone ringing. He quickly diverts his attention away from the road down to the screen.

"Are you going to take that?" I ask him. "I don't mind."

"Ah, it's just a random girl I slept with the other night," Drake says as he rejects the call. "That's my burner phone ringing. I give that number out to girls and I never answer it. See, you can have girls, Bishop. Just don't let them come between you and the music."

I let out a disapproving scoff. "Man, you're worse than me."

"We all have our vices, Bishop. Mine is just never giving a shit about any relationship longer than a night."

"As you keep reminding everyone. You do you," I say.

"So, what are you going to do now that Chloe is in town for the next few days?" Drake asks me. "What's the big plan?"

"I'm gonna find her."

"Oh, yeah?"

"What do you think? Should I give Lucas a call?"

"Why would you call our manager?" he asks me.

I turn to Drake and roll my eyes like he's an idiot. "Because he knows how to find anyone in this city. Even someone who doesn't want to be found by me."

"And what, pray I ask, are you going to do when Lucas finds her?"

I dig into my pocket for my phone. I pull up Lucas' number on the contacts list. "I don't know what I'm going to do," I reply. "But I've certainly got unfinished business with her."

# 10

*CHLOE*

"So, tell me about you," Gary says from the opposite side of the booth. He leans forward and rests his head on his hands, placing all his focus on me. "I gotta make sure I don't have some lunatic staying with me who might murder me in my sleep."

I shift nervously in my seat. "What do you want to know?"

Gary's eyes sparkle. "Everything, Chloe. *Everything*."

I let out an anxious giggle. "There's not much to know, really."

Gary raises his eyebrows like he doesn't believe me. "Well, you're clearly super talented and incredibly beautiful. I'm sure there's more to you than meets the eye. I am sure you have some stories under there."

I blush. Gary is definitely a hell of a lot of fun already, and I've only known him for an hour.

He's taken me to a bar just a block away from his apartment. He told me, on the way, that it's a place he takes dates to, but that I shouldn't be worried. I'm not his type. Mainly because I don't have a dick.

His words, not mine.

"There might be some stories," I reply conspiratorially.

Gary smiles at that. He calls a server over and flirts outrageously with her before ordering our first drinks.

"We need two *very* strong Sex on the Beaches, please. More alcohol than juice if you know what I mean. I want to get my friend here to loosen up and talk about her illustrious life, so we need those drinks to be as strong as they can be."

He winks at the server.

"Oh no, Gary."

"Oh yes, Chloe."

"Well, I can pay for these if we're going to drown them," I say, already pulling out my empty card.

"Oh, no. This is going to be all me," Gary replies with a dismissive wave. "I'm taking you out for a good night, Chloe, so it's my shout, plus it's my town and I've got to show you the good side of it."

"If you insist."

"Oh, I very much insist."

When the cocktails arrive at our table, we clink glasses and immediately Gary is back on the interrogation.

"Talking about sex on the beach, tell me about your love life, Chloe."

I nearly spurt out my drink.

"You can't ask a lady a question like that, Gary," I say in mock disbelief.

"I'm the one buying drinks, remember? You owe me some juicy details, at the very least."

I shrug. "You've got me there."

Gary leans back in close. "Is there a man in the picture? Please tell me he's tall, dark, and handsome..."

"There's been some guys."

"You're going to have to do better than that, Chloe. Don't tell me I have to buy you another drink to wring it out of you."

I take a long sip of the cocktail. For Dutch courage.

"There is – *was* – a boy," I start.

"Oh, I'm already liking where this is going. Tell me more. Don't stop."

"He was a boy I got with when I was in high school."

"Cute," Gary replies. "Continue."

"There was a *slight* problem, though. He was one of the best friends of my brother."

Gary leans back with a satisfied grin. "Juicy, Chloe. You bad girl. I'm loving this."

"We kept it all hidden from my brother, though..."

"*Very* juicy."

"But then he did something that shattered me and my confidence for a long time. Something that's taken years to heal. There have been a few flings since him, but nothing compares to your first love, don't they? Especially when you were teenagers when it happened. All those hormones and new emotions..."

"My first love was a Puerto Rican guy I met while traveling through Brazil," Gary says. "He taught me things that I didn't know existed, so I completely understand."

"It wasn't exactly like that."

"No?"

Gary summons over the server again and orders another round of drinks.

"You're really going to get me drunk super fast," I tell him. "I'm such a lightweight."

"That's exactly the point," Gary replies with a smirk. "This is going to be *fun*."

More cocktails come and I'm downing them like a

Viking. Gary recounts all these stories of sexual encounters he's had. It seems like he's slept with half of the West Coast and tried every position under the sun.

The bar is loud and packed to the rafters. It's a popular spot and I can see why Gary brings all his dates here. The vibe is cool, and the music is thumping.

But it's only a matter of time before the music fades.

And the karaoke starts.

I didn't notice the stage on the other side of the bar when we entered, but now I very much do. There's a screen, microphone stand, jukebox, and everything. All you need to embarrass yourself in front of a room full of strangers.

"Holy shit, karaoke."

I gulp and avert my eyes from the whole setup in the corner.

Gary, on the other hand, is thrilled about it. He claps and squeals. "You should definitely put your name in for a turn, Chloe."

"No freaking way."

"Come on, with your talent you'll blow everyone's socks off. Guaran-*fucking*-teed."

"Nope. Karaoke isn't for me, Gary."

"Oh yes, it is. You've got the most amazing voice," Gary replies. "If I were you, I'd be singing all day long. If I had your voice, people would have to tape my mouth to shut me up. You must try karaoke."

"No, Gary."

"Okay, I'm going to order a round of shots. Then we'll see."

Before I can protest, he's already got the server over.

"What kind of shots?" I ask Gary warily, but he's already speaking to the server he's been flirting with all night.

"Look through your liquor for the bottle with the highest alcohol percentage. That's what I want. I'm assuming it'll be some kind of tequila."

The server leaves, and my head is in my hands.

"Oh no, Gary."

"This will get you in the mood for some singing. I need to hear you live, girl, if you're going to be staying in my apartment. Consider it my down payment."

"I promise you I'm not singing, Gary."

"How can you follow your dreams when you can't even sing drunk in some random bar?"

I sigh.

"Fine. Whatever. I'll give it a go."

Gary's face lights up like a Christmas tree. "That's the spirit, girl."

The shots come. Tequila, of course. Proper Mexican heavy-duty stuff. We sink them quickly and then I'm practically pushed onto the karaoke stage by Gary.

Before I know it, I'm facing the bar and freaking out.

*Okay, pick a song, Chloe.*

I type in Landslide by Fleetwood Mac. I used to always sing this song with my brother when we were kids in the living room. I know it so well.

The familiar opening chords begin to play, and I turn to look out at the audience. It's been a long time since I've performed live. Everyone seems to be staring at me. Gary is staring at me.

They want me to sing.

But I don't.

I don't sing a word.

I'm vulnerable. Alone. Exposed up here on stage.

Those... feelings of what happened come rushing back and there's a voice in the back of my head that repeats over and over, louder and louder, until it's screaming.

*I'm going to screw this all up.*

Bishop did this to me. He was the one who made me unable to ever sing in public again. He tipped me over the edge all those years ago, and he did it deliberately.

I'm unable to perform live because of him. Because of the fear he instilled in me.

I act like I'm in a dream and immediately walk straight off the stage.

I stand at the back of the bar with my back turned to the audience. The chords of Landslide continue to play with no words.

I can't leave it like this. This is all my nightmares coming back to haunt me at once.

I have no choice. I have to prove it to myself that I can perform live. I have to prove to myself that Bishop doesn't hold that power over me. It's been seven years. I don't have to be enthralled to that man anymore.

*I am better than this.*

"Come on, Chloe," I whisper to myself. "This is your passion. Let's kick some ass."

A deep breath. And then another. The screaming voice in my head dissolves.

And I'm going back on the stage, heading straight for the microphone...

And I start to sing.

And it's good. I'm actually alright. No one is booing me. No one is laughing.

*I can do this.*

Everything goes blurry, and it's like I'm back in my bedroom performing just in front of the camera. Back to performing with Axel in our living room in front of our TV. No memories of Bishop. No audience in the karaoke bar. No Gary. No fear.

And then it's the end of the song.

I step off the stage, overwhelmed. Someone approaches and I'm assuming it's Gary handing me another strong cocktail.

But the first face I see is Bishop's.

*This isn't a hallucination. He's here. In front of me.*

"Wow," Ravaged's guitarist says. "That was *great*, Chloe."

And somehow, for the second time in one night, he's found me.

# 11

SEVEN YEARS AGO

*CHLOE*

"I GET nervous when I perform live. I've tried everything, but it's always just... *there*. I hate it. I hate it. I hate it."

Bishop leans in close, disbelief in his frown as he looks at me.

"What do you mean?" he asks. "Explain what happens."

I take in a big inhale of air. "When I go in front of people, I just think about how they're all watching me. Judging me. Laughing at me. And then I can't get the words out. It's like it overwhelms all my senses and I just feel worthless. I have had this fear all my life and no matter how many times I try to get rid of it, I can't. I've been able to perform live a few times, but it's hard. I'm worried that one mishap... one issue on stage... and maybe I will never want to perform live again."

It's a big admission to make, even if it is to the man I'm falling in love with. The only person who I've ever been brave enough to talk to about my fear is Axel.

It sounds so ridiculous, hearing it said out loud. So freaking childish. Why would I want to be a rockstar when I can get absolutely terrified of even showcasing my talent in front of others? It just doesn't make sense, but it's the truth. I get super nervous when I perform live. Simple as that.

Bishop kisses me.

"Nonsense," he whispers as he strokes my cheek, calming me down. He's always able to soothe me. It's like his superpower.

We're sitting on my bed, my door closed. We're yet again hiding Bishop's presence from my family, and especially my brother next door.

"Your kisses always make me feel better," I reply, closing my eyes. "Your kisses make me forget the world outside this room."

The man leans back. "You need to learn not to be so nervous when you perform, Chloe," he says. "You need to get over that fear."

"I can't."

"Look, I took the risk sneaking in here today in order to help you practice for Drake's audition, and now I know that things may be harder than they first appear, but I'm going to see you on that stage in front of Drake and whoever's going to be there. You're going to be fucking amazing. You're going to be a rockstar, remember that."

"Okay."

"We can do it, Chloe. *You* can do it."

He's so passionate about the idea of helping me play that he raises his voice. I place a finger over his mouth and hush him quickly.

"Be careful or Axel will hear you. He'll recognize your voice."

Bishop sniggers.

"Oh, he'll kill me if he ever found out I was in here screwing his sister."

I slap him on the shoulder.

"Stop it, Bishop."

He takes my chin in his fingers and draws me in for another long kiss.

"I like this being so forbidden," he says. "Makes you seem so much more irresistible."

"Shut up."

"Do you know how much I think about you?"

I can't resist. "How much?"

"All the fucking time."

"Really?"

"I have *dreams* about you, Chloe."

"I dream about you too."

"And what happens in those dreams?"

I smirk. "Wouldn't you like to know?"

"Very much so, yes. Especially if they're anywhere near as naughty as the dreams I have about you... and your body."

"Now you really need to shut up."

Bishop places his hand on my leg and slowly glides up towards my sensitive parts. I let him do so. I let him reach the rim of my pants before I slap his wandering hand away.

"We need to focus," I admonish him. "Stop being cheeky."

He grunts. Denied.

"Have you picked a song for Drake's audition yet?" he asks me.

I bite my lip.

*I gotta tell him now.*

"Yep," I reply nervously. "I was thinking of doing the song I wrote for you."

Bishop just smiles at me with the goofiest grin on the planet. He doesn't say anything.

"What?" I ask him, hesitant.

"You're fucking beautiful, you know that?"

My cheeks burn, but I know we must remain on task. I don't think I have the willpower to resist his hand a second time.

"Bishop, I'm so nervous about doing this I feel sick. Maybe you should do it instead..."

"No," he replies. "You need to do this. It'll be good for you."

I nod. "Okay."

"How about you perform the song now?" he asks. "Just for me?"

And I do.

* * *

I GENTLY PLACE my trusty guitar back on the bed and turn to Bishop.

"That was good," he says. "Really good. If you do *that* on stage, then I bet Drake will be offering you a place on the spot, no question at all."

"You think?"

"I *know*, Chloe."

I take in a deep breath, readying to say what's been weighing heavily on my mind. It's taking me a lot of courage to speak up about this.

*Here it comes.*

"Bishop?"

He senses the tension in my voice. "Yeah?"

"I'm considering telling Axel about us."

Silence.

"Seriously?"

"Yes."

Bishop's immediate reaction is to shake his head. "You can't, Chloe."

"We can't keep continuing to sneak around, Bishop. It's not good. I can't keep lying to my brother, I just can't."

"Your loyalty is an admirable trait," he says. "You are the most loyal person I know. I like that about you. But Chloe, you're going to take it too far."

"I'm loyal to my brother," I say. "Sneaking around like this is fun and sexy and whatever, but it goes against my instinct. I'm sorry, but we have to tell him."

"You know Axel will kill me, right? I'm a dead man walking."

"When should we tell him, then?"

Bishop shrugs. "Never, preferably."

I roll my eyes. "That's not being realistic."

"I might tell Axel at the altar."

I cross my arms. "That's a bad joke."

Bishop sighs and motions for me to sit down next to him on the bed.

"I'm sorry, Chloe, but we can't tell him."

"And what if Axel sniffs out something?" I ask. "What do I say then? It will be worse if he catches us together than if I just break it to him carefully. It might even be better if you tell him."

Bishop snorts derisively. "That'll be hilarious."

"What do we do, Bishop?"

"We say nothing. You say nothing. It's the wrong idea to tell him. The last thing I need, or want, is Axel finding out and having to deal with all that. Axel will drive us apart. There's no doubt about that. He will kill me. I don't want to lose a friendship. I don't want to choose between you or him."

"That's all just unfounded. How do you know he'll react like that?"

Bishop takes a long pause before he speaks again. "Ever since Gabe passed away, Axel and I have grown really close." Gabe was Axel's best friend from childhood who died from a bad fight with cancer a few years ago. It was traumatic, to say the least. I still remember walking in on Axel crying in his bedroom when he returned from the hospital for the last time, trying so hard to hide his uncontrollable grief from the two women in his family. That image will be seared on my mind for the rest of my life. My cool older brother reduced to sobs as his childhood best friend passed away. Bishop was there to be a comforting friend to Axel. Nothing binds people together more than shared grief.

"I know," I reply softly. "You've done so much for Axel."

"I can't do this to my best friend," Bishop says. "I'm sleeping with his little sister. If he found out, then it'll ruin everything we have together."

"Yeah."

Bishop looks sad. He looks like he's close to tears. I bet he's remembering Gabe and those awful times as well.

We both have those memories.

"I'm not ready for my best friend to know about us," he continues. "Please don't tell him, Chloe."

"Okay," I reply, but there's no conviction in my voice.

I still have my worries.

# 12

*BISHOP*

I STARE into Chloe's gorgeous green eyes as she suddenly realizes I *am* real and that I *am* actually standing in front of her at the edge of the karaoke stage. I see the flicker of recognition pass through her expression.

And then her *holy shit* moment.

Man, these are the moments I relish.

*Yeah, girl, I'm here and I'm fucking real.*

The loudness of the bar seems to fade away, and it feels like it's only Chloe and me. Standing inches apart. Eyes locked. Time slips away, and it's like I'm just snuck through her bedroom window again.

"What the hell are you doing here?" she asks me, her voice sharpening as if breaking out of a daze. "What do you think you're doing?"

"Like I said," I reply, unable to resist the smirk on my face. "That was great, Chloe. You're better than great, in fact. You are even better than I remember."

She looks taken aback by that comment, but only for the

briefest of seconds before she's back in her *fuck Bishop* attitude. Those pretty green eyes of hers narrow and she stabs a threatening finger in my direction.

She looks like her brother when she's angry.

"I'm going to ask you again, Bishop. What the *hell* are you doing here?"

"To see you, of course."

She bristles at that.

Oh, how I love making her livid. She scrunches up her pretty face and glares at me after my snide response. I love how much effort she's putting into hating my guts. It means she cares. She could've stormed off the moment she bumped into me just then. She could've simply slapped me and walked away from my face, but she's still trying to coax the mystery out of me, and that means that somewhere, deep down, she's still got something for me.

*I never lose.*

"How have you found me?" she asks, her voice rising to a fever pitch.

"Don't act so confused, Chloe," I reply calmly. "I'm an international rockstar worth millions. Of course I have the resources to easily find a girl in Los Angeles. I mean, you're not exactly in witness protection or anything."

She crosses her arms, and that's when I realize that she's a bit tipsy. She must've engulfed a whole shipment of drinks to gather the confidence to do that karaoke. But, even drunk and swaying on her feet, she still has that grit I saw from her outside Axel and Maddie's place a few hours ago.

I'm glad I spoke to Lucas and got him and his team to track her down.

She looks amazing right now. She's applied ruby red lipstick and her black hair hangs down carefree. She's made herself up for a good night out, and I've come here to ruin it in the most dramatic fashion. It's so much fun.

"You need to leave," she tells me bluntly.

"Nope."

"I said to you literally an hour ago that I don't want to see you again, yet here you are at this random bar, here to see me. What a complete reversal. Can't one simple instruction get through your dumb skull, Bishop, or are you just stupid?"

"Lots of mean words there that I'm going to ignore," I say. I nod up to the microphone. "It's crazy you haven't gone viral before with the talent you just displayed."

"I usually choke up in public, don't you remember?"

"I do," I say. "I remember that day when you did."

"Yeah," Chloe replies bitterly. "I would hope you wouldn't have forgotten the day you broke my heart."

"Ah. That's what all this is about?"

"Just go, Bishop. Leave me alone and live your fancy rockstar life."

I lean in close so that I can smell her. Chloe's sweet perfume fills my nose. I wish for nothing more than to take her now in my arms and kiss her until she gives into me. "I've thought about it long and hard," I say. "And I've come to the conclusion that I can't live my rockstar life if you aren't in it."

I am putting my heart on the line, and Chloe merely scoffs. "We're really having a repeat of what happened outside my brother's? Now? You're stupider than you look, Bishop. When can you get this all through your thick brain? You expect me to just forget everything that's gone on between us, then? Forget the past seven years haven't existed? Drop my entire life for you simply because you're a horny bastard who wants to ruin me again?"

"If I were simply horny, then there are a million ways I can solve that right now," I reply quietly. "I just want you. I'm not going to give up until I have you. I'll *never* give up."

"Tough, because you can't have me," Chloe whispers back. "I'm living my own life."

I nod. I'm not giving in that easily. "I feel like fate has drawn us together tonight, Chloe. Out of all the million places I could've been tonight, I ended up with you."

"It wasn't fate, Bishop. It was me coming across the country to see my brother. That's all."

"I know you want closure with me, so why not let me give that to you?"

Chloe laughs then. She doesn't believe me at all.

*Man, I'm really having to fight for her trust, aren't I?*

And there's no guarantee I'm going to get it.

"Closure sounds a lot like you having sex with me."

"It's much more than that, Chloe."

"You're disgusting. I'm not yours anymore. Not since what happened."

I really want to answer her. I want to lay everything out for her. I'm doing what I told Drake back in the car I never do. Begging.

I'm trying to erase the past. I'm trying to show the woman I once fell in love with that I've changed.

But before I can say another word, some large guy jumps in between Chloe and me.

*Who the fuck's this fuck?*

"What's going on, Chloe?" the man asks her, ignoring me.

"Who the hell is this guy?" I ask the girl over the big guy's shoulder. "Your new fling? The secret boyfriend you're hiding?"

I'm not jealous if she does have some guy.

Okay... maybe I'm a *little* bit jealous. I am human, after all.

But hopefully, this guy isn't hers. Please God, I hope he isn't her man.

"This is the guy I was talking about," Chloe says to maybe-new-boyfriend, disregarding my questions. "My ex."

His head swivels around from her to me and then back to her, acknowledging my presence for the first time with his eyes.

"Not the guy from your past?"

Chloe crosses her arms. "Yep."

"You were talking about me?" I ask.

*Oh, this is a development. A boost to my crusade.*

The guy waves at me. "Back off from Chloe."

*Wait... is he threatening me?*

I'm not having that. I'm twice his size in height and muscles.

This is funny. Real fucking funny.

"Who the fuck is this guy, Chloe? Answer me before I knock him out. I swear to God."

"Come home with me," the guy says to Chloe. "Leave him."

"Hang on," she replies. "I want to say one more thing to Bishop."

I would really love to give this random dude a good beating, but I would rather hear what Chloe has to say. "What is it?"

She squeezes past the guy and takes a step right up to my face. We're nose to nose, and not in a good way. "Everything difficult in my life is due to what you did to me all those years ago," she says.

"Maybe I'm not completely to blame," I say. "You were also involved."

"So you're never going to apologize for what you did?" she asks me.

"No."

"I might've forgiven you," Chloe says. "Once. When it happened."

"Well, that time has clearly passed," I say. "But I've never stopped loving you, Chloe. I've never stopped thinking about you. Every single fucking day."

She pauses for a moment. I just know my words have an impact on her. I can see it in her beautiful green eyes.

"You're toxic," she eventually replies.

And then she turns to go. She nods at her friend to follow. I haven't realized, but he's been staring at me this whole time.

"Wait," he says. "Aren't you..."

"Bishop Hayes," Chloe finishes for him. "Yep. It's him. The famous rockstar, and the biggest asshole on planet Earth."

And then she truly goes. Leaving me once again standing there watching her back.

# 13

*CHLOE*

I BREAK DOWN. I give in. I go against all advice given to me by seemingly everyone I know.

I decide to check the view count and read the comments on my viral video.

Of course, I instantly realize it's a mistake.

*Wow.*

Sure, the numbers are good – well, more than good. They're *off-the-wall* crazy. Nearly ten million views in a couple of days. But the first comment I see is one aimed solely at my appearance.

I resemble a goblin, apparently.

The next comment is simply about how shit my voice is.

And that's when I throw my phone against the wall. It lands with a wimpy thud on the carpet. I'm even shit at angrily throwing stuff.

*Well, I'm not making that mistake to check the comments ever again.*

To vent out all that weird negative energy, I do the one thing that brings me inner peace.

I pick up my guitar and start playing.

It's not only the comments I need exorcising, but I also need to get a whole load of practice in before this big meeting with Mickey Miller tomorrow. Getting drunk and letting my hair down at the bar last night was not a good idea in hindsight. Now I'm even more nervous and trying to manage a thumping headache of a hangover. I really should've just spent yesterday evening going over my songs again and again.

I'm sitting in Gary's living room. He's left this morning for work, happy as a puppy. That man did not have a hangover, it seems.

What if the big shot producer makes me sing in front of him? What if he, like the anonymous online critic, thinks I have a shit voice? No wonder I've kept my music just to myself all these years when my head is filled with doubts like these. The pressure for tomorrow is freaking intense.

I go over one of my songs once. Twice. Three times. Improving it. Familiarizing myself with it once again. The more I play, the more confident I feel. The less the doubts in my head yell at me. That's me, persistent Chloe.

*I can do this. I've done this for most of my life. Why do I disregard my talent all the freaking time?*

When I finish playing it for the fifth time, there's a knock at the door. This isn't my apartment, so I don't know whether I should open it, but then I hear a voice.

"Chloe, I know you're in there. I can hear you playing."

I know who that is.

I leap up from the couch and open the door to Maddie, standing there with a beaming smile on her face.

"Hello," I greet.

"Hi! Sorry, I could overhear you playing. That sounded really good."

"Thanks," I blush.

"I hope I'm not intruding, but Axel gave me the address where you're staying. I thought you might need a friendly face in Los Angeles today, so I've brought some of my cookies."

She holds up a Tupperware box full of the addictive sugary things. My mouth waters at the sight of choc chips.

"That is a godsend, Maddie. Thank you. Come on in."

Maddie looks around the apartment. "Cute place."

"Oh, the guy who lives here is super cool and so funny. He took me out for drinks last night."

"Making friends already? That's great."

"Seems like," I reply, looking over Maddie's shoulder at the empty doorway. "Where's my brother? He didn't escort you here?"

"Oh, Ravaged has got a one-off secret performance tonight in some basement bar for a hundred fans. It's a charity thing. They're getting ready for it."

"Oh, right."

*That's where Bishop would be.*

Why do my thoughts instantly go to him? I don't want to be thinking about him. Not now, not ever.

"Are you going to see it?" I ask her.

"I won't. I'd rather give up my ticket to a fan," she replies. "Plus, I wanted to come and say hi to my baby's new auntie."

I smile at that. "You want anything?" I ask. "Juice? Coffee?"

"Just a glass of water."

"Well, I'm going to try one of these cookies," I say, reaching into the Tupperware box. When that taste hits my lips, I let out a satisfied moan. "Still freaking amazing, Maddie."

"How are you feeling about tomorrow with the producer?" she asks me as we take a seat on Gary's couch and I hand her the water.

"I'm not going to lie to you, Maddie. I'm freaking out."

"Can I hear you sing? Properly and not through a door, if that's alright? I'm no musician, but I guess performing in front of someone is good, no?"

*Any practice is good practice.*

"Yeah, okay."

I pick up my guitar and start playing the song I was just practicing. Maddie nods along to it, smiling encouragingly.

But I only get halfway through the song before I have to stop.

"I'm not feeling it," I excuse, not wanting to get into the real reason I can't do anything live in front of someone.

I can't do it when she's right there looking at me like that. Looking at me like she's in awe. I feel like a fraud.

I just can't do it.

"You sound great, really," Maddie replies, her hand on my knee. "You should continue. I would like to hear the rest."

"I should save my voice for tomorrow," I lie.

"Okay."

"I know you just said you're no musician," I start, trying to change the subject. "But do you play anything? Sing? Dance?"

Maddie scoffs. "No. I wish. No one should hear me sing and I'm absolutely terrible with my feet and rhythm. I'm more than happy to simply watch talented people like you and Axel."

I laugh. "And how's the pregnancy coming along?"

Maddie rubs her not-showing belly. "Everything hurts.

My boobs ache. I can't remember the last time I had a shit. And, worse of all, I can't even have a drink to help ease all the nerves. But this is the most amazing, miraculous, and magical thing to ever happen to me, and I would not take the surprise of it back for all the money in the world. Even if I'm randomly craving cinnamon donuts all the freaking time. Although I don't know if any of that is because of the pregnancy or just because I'm a moody person."

She's so cute that I just reach over and give her a big hug. "I can't believe you're going to be part of our family," I say.

"Me too," Maddie replies. "When you came over yesterday, I instantly knew I was going to get on well with you."

"Yesterday seems like a lifetime ago," I reply. "I'm sorry that I kinda just skipped out on you two."

Maddie narrows her eyes. "Look, I know this isn't my place, but is there something going on between you and Bishop Hayes?" she asks quietly. I can tell she's been waiting to ask this the minute she walked in through the door. "I tried to speak to Axel about what happened between you all yesterday, but he's not saying a word to me. My Spidey Sense is tingling. I don't mean to pry, though. It's just that you could cut the tension yesterday with a knife, and I would have to be an idiot to not see something..."

"It's okay," I reply. I trust Maddie. "Bishop and I go back... a long way."

"Ah."

"We were both teenagers in love."

Maddie nods. "I suspected as much."

"We hid it from my brother and everything."

"So you met through Axel?"

"Yeah."

"Oh, that must've been so much fun," Maddie giggles.

"All those taboo glances across the room. Secret looks in hallways."

I shake my head. "Yeah, it was a lot of fun. At first."

"And then what happened?"

"I thought we were going to be together forever. Maybe I was just being a naïve teenage girl who's watched too many Disney princess movies, but I really did think he was the one for me. But then he acted like a total dick and ruined my self-confidence for a very, very long time."

I don't want to go into the details with her, so I tell her what she needs to know. The abridged version of events.

"Well, he clearly still likes you, Chloe," Maddie replies softly. "I saw how he acted with you yesterday. But if he's been shit to you in the past, then screw him. Did he apologize for what he did to you?"

"Nope."

"Then, really, *fuck* him."

We both fall into a burst of shared laughter.

"I'm guessing my brother wasn't the easiest guy to fall in love with," I remark to my new sister.

"Oh." Maddie gives me the funniest look. "He was a *nightmare*."

"Really?"

"But that's men for you," she replies. "You can't help but love them, despite all their faults. Sometimes they do know exactly how to treat you like a Disney princess, and then you're falling for them against your better judgment. And then sometimes you do get your happy ever after, and it's the best thing."

I sigh in resignation and reach into Maddie's Tupperware.

"I don't think I'll get my happy ever after," I say. "But I will help myself to another cookie. That's close enough."

# 14

*BISHOP*

It's a damn good thing that Ravaged is performing tonight because otherwise I might do something crazy.

Like find Chloe again.

And maybe even talk to her.

*Yeah, that would be crazy.*

Performing music is the one thing that clears my head during times of crisis, and it's definitely a time of crisis right now. My head needs a whole spring clean. It's all to do with my best friend's sister. Chloe has been a permanent fixture on my mind since she appeared out of nowhere yesterday at Axel's place like a surprise summer tropical storm wrecking everything in her path. I had thought I was strong, that I was over her, that I wouldn't quake in her presence if I saw her again, but I was so very wrong.

*She's still so damn beautiful.*

I must have her again.

Everything is about her.

But performing on stage here in this small basement bar

to a select group of fans is where I feel like I can just let go of all the fucking *stress* that's built up in me for the last day. I'm in my element here. As I play, I look around at the other members of Ravaged performing along with me. I look out at the crowd with their adoring faces. This isn't a big arena that we've become accustomed to. This is an intimate charity gig. Just us boys, the music, and a small crowd. *This* is important.

The set is great. The audience is great. The music is banging.

And I feel like I can finally relax.

After the show, us boys take our seats at the back of the bar and have a round of drinks to cool down. Drake has a new girl around his arm, as usual. I give him a roll of my eyes before I order a very expensive glass of Scotch for myself.

Caspian, Ravaged's drummer, leans in to me as I take my first sip. "You okay?"

The man is massive. Pure muscle. His wide shoulders practically take up two seats. He barely speaks anything more than a syllable at a time, so him asking me if I'm okay means a serious amount of concern.

"I'm fine," I reply. "Why do you ask?"

Caspian shrugs and grunts. "You seem different today."

Drake giggles like a schoolchild. He's obviously over-heard us. "Bishop saw Chloe yesterday for the first time since Crystal River," he pipes up. The girl sitting on his lap trails a seductive finger down the middle of his chest.

"Shit." That's Caspian's reply. He sums up the situation perfectly.

I look for Axel, afraid he might also be overhearing this little fucked-up conversation. He's busy in the corner having a conversation with Lucas, our manager. Good.

"And how do you feel about that?" Drake asks me, ignoring the fawning girl trying to get his attention.

"We've moved past all that," I mutter. I want to move on past this conversation if I'm being honest. Fuck Drake's poking. "We're all adults now."

"You didn't like it when she rejected you, didn't you?" Drake teases.

"I would have my hands wrapped around your neck if there wasn't a girl in the way, Drake."

Caspian laughs at that as the girl whispers in Drake's ear.

"She wants to tell you something," Drake says to me, nodding to the woman who can't get enough of him. "Come here."

I sigh and lean in towards them.

Drake's girl is gorgeous, but clearly one of those clout-chasing Instagram influencers who we've come to be very familiar with being a famous rockstar band. They slide into our beds, pussies wet, for little more than a glance in their direction. Pussy becomes cheap when you're an international rockstar. That's why, when a real girl like Chloe or Maddie comes along, you take them as fast as you can. That's a lesson I should've learned seven years ago.

"What is it?" I ask both my band's lead singer and the clout-chaser.

The woman admires my body up and down with a flick of her eyes. She bites her lip. "You're *so* good-looking," she whispers.

Ah. This is what she wanted to tell me. Drake's hilarious.

"I know that," I reply.

"I've got a friend I can bring over right now. A friend who I think you'll like. She's a bad girl who likes bad boys like you."

Her voice is deep and sultry. At any other time and place, I would say something witty in the affirmative.

But not tonight. Not when Chloe is on my mind.

"No."

"That's a first," Drake remarks, watching the girl and my interaction with a cheeky grin. "So, you're definitely still hung over Axel's little sister, huh?"

"You're gonna have to be careful with where you're going with that," I warn him. "If I don't beat you up for talking about Axel's sister, then Caspian certainly will."

"Yep," comes the reply from behind me. Caspian's been watching. No one disrespects a family member of Ravaged, even Drake.

The lead singer of Ravaged slaps me on the hand. "I'm just messing, Bishop."

I scowl at him and lean back into my seat.

We drink together for the next half-hour, chatting about the performance. Drake's the first to leave, the girl practically drooling over him.

"Have a good night," I tell him as he leaves with her. "Enjoy."

He shakes my hand and whispers into my ear. "No offense meant, Bishop."

"None taken."

"Go after her," he tells me before he walks out the door. "But don't you dare forget about what the number one priority is."

I roll my eyes. "Ravaged, I know."

"Good boy."

"Fuck off and get your dick wet."

Then it's Caspian's turn to go. Giving me a fist bump and a grunt as a farewell.

Leaving just Axel and me sitting together.

We sit in silence for a moment as I finish my drink.

*Please don't mention Chloe. Please don't mention Chloe. Please don't mention Chloe.*

But then Axel speaks.

"I know it's not my place, Bishop, but I think you should talk to Chloe."

*Fuck.*

"This is not a joke, right? You're not going to kill me for daring to say her name?"

"No, Bishop, I'm not planning on killing you for talking about my little sister. Yet."

I take in a deep breath. We've not spoken about his little sister for a very long time, so this is clearly coming from his heart, and I know how hard it is for Axel to speak emotionally. Hell, a few months ago he was a worse playboy than even Drake, known for his *Active Axel* nickname and partying personality. But then Maddie entered the picture and changed the man into a better version of himself. He had been living a life that was empty, but then Maddie showed him the truth.

And now he wants to talk about Chloe.

And he wants me to actually fucking *talk* to her.

"That's what I'm trying to do," I tell my best friend. "But, in case you didn't know, she hates me. She's made that *very* clear."

Axel raises an eyebrow. "Really?"

"Yes, really."

"I know my own sister, Bishop. I know she'll give you one more chance, even if she won't admit it herself. She still likes you, trust me."

"I doubt it."

Axel smiles and shakes his head. "Oh, she does. She's just not going to give in easily. She's a strong girl who knows herself and her boundaries, but are you the man who gives up at the first sign of pushback? Really? You?"

97

"No, I'm not," I reply forcefully. "I never give up."

"So, Bishop, you know what you have to do, then. You're just really gonna have to work for her. Let's talk about this outside. I want to speak to you in private, away from prying eyes."

*Oh shit.*

# 15

SEVEN YEARS AGO

*CHLOE*

I CAN'T BEAR it anymore.

I need to tell Axel.

This illusion that Bishop and I are pulling over my brother's eyes can only last for so long before he finds out one way or another, and if Bishop doesn't want to tell him, then I will. The idea of it is eating me up. He needs to know, and it needs to come from me, before he discovers things for himself and it all gets ugly.

I take in a deep breath and try to calm myself as I stand in front of my brother's door. I build up enough courage to knock. Axel has his bedroom door already open, but I want to get his attention before I stumble in.

I can see my brother. He's got his headphones on, listening to music as he plays on his bass guitar. He's been practicing all the time, and I can hear the improvement.

The man eats, sleeps, and breathes music. It's kinda cute how we share the same passion. It makes us close, but also causes the biggest arguments. We are so alike that we're light flames burning each other.

He spots me standing awkwardly in his doorway. Axel removes his headphones and blinks at me.

"Chloe?"

"Can we talk?" I ask him, so much more formally than we ever are.

"Sure. Take a seat."

I sit down on the only available seat. His bed. Suddenly, I don't know what to do with my hands. I'm so nervous that I've become super self-conscious. I place them in my lap, squeezing my fingers together. Axel doesn't seem to notice my bubbling anxiety.

"How's the audition prep for Drake's band going?" I ask him.

Axel nods. "Yeah, good. Just perfecting everything."

"I'm always hearing you from my room."

"You're planning to do the audition too, right? That's what Bishop's told me."

*Bishop. What has he said? That we've talked? Is he flying too close to the sun? That cocky bastard...*

"Why would you hear that from Bishop?" I ask, faking innocence.

Axel waves his hand dismissively. "I think he said he heard it from one of the girls at school."

"Right. Well, yeah, he's heard it correctly. I am considering doing the audition."

Axel's face lights up. "That would be sick. Imagine us two together in a band. It would be so cool."

I gulp. I can't put it off any longer.

"There's something I got to tell you," I say, my voice breaking.

"What is it?"

"It's going to sound bad at first, so I don't want you to have a bad reaction."

Axel goes quiet. He knows when I'm no longer joking around and when I'm serious. "Okay…"

"Promise me you won't get mad."

"I can't make that promise."

"Please, Axel."

"Fine. I promise I won't go mad."

I close my eyes.

And then I say it.

"Bishop and I have been seeing each other."

Axel snorts.

"What do you mean, *seeing*?"

"Like, dating. Secretly."

He laughs. "You're joking, aren't you?"

"I'm not."

"Because that'll be a weird-ass thing to joke about, Chloe, especially coming out of the blue. You and Bishop? Seriously?"

I stare at him solemnly. "I'm not joking, Axel. We've been seeing each other."

Silence.

"For how long?" he asks me, his voice already hardening.

*Please don't react bad. Please don't react bad. Please don't react bad.*

"A few months."

My brother simply glares at me, everything I've just said finally sinking in. He doesn't say a thing.

I can't tell what he's thinking, but I know it ain't good. He's going to explode. He's going to go mad; I just know it.

"Don't kill him," I whisper. "Please. You promised not to go mad."

Axel clenches his jaw and I see him change in front of my eyes into a man hell-bent on violence.

I see his promise not to flip mad break in front of my eyes.

"I'm going to kill that son of a bitch."

# 16

*BISHOP*

"FOLLOW ME TO MY CAR," Axel commands ominously.

*Am I about to be bitch slapped?*

"Sure."

He's taking me away from other people literally after we've been speaking about me fucking his sister, so of course I'm a tad worried. Even if he's promised not to kill me.

*That could've been a fib.*

Goodbye, cruel world.

We leave the basement bar via the back entrance to not attract the crowd outside. We members of Ravaged have become very used to sneaking out of the back of buildings now that we're some of the most famous faces on earth. It's one of the tradeoffs for our incredible lives.

I'm still wary of my best friend. Sure, he says that Chloe will give me another chance, but I remember the way he reacted the time his sister told him about us, and I don't want a repeat of what happened then.

We step outside in the warm Los Angeles night air. I spot Axel's motorbike parked across the street. His beloved Kawasaki. What a beast of a ride. It's just us here now. No one around to witness a murder.

Axel hasn't spoken a word on our way out, but now he turns to me, a serious, somber expression on his face.

*Oh shit. Here it comes.*

"Do you truly love Chloe?" he asks in a straight, blunt tone. He's been building up to asking me this in his head, I see.

I sigh. We're gonna have this out here, then. There's no escaping.

I'm not going to lie to my best friend. I once kept a big secret from him and look how that turned out, so I swore never again.

"Isn't it obvious that I do love her? I've always loved her," I say.

"Are you bullshitting me?" Axel asks.

"I truly am not," I reply. "Chloe has been the only girl I've ever loved. In my eyes, she's the most beautiful girl in the world, and always has been. You're not going to attempt to beat me up for that, are you?"

Chloe's brother pauses.

"I'll beat you up if you don't go and get her."

"Okay."

"I know you both, and I know that Chloe brings out the best in you. You better do this, Bishop, and you better do it right."

I pat my best friend on the shoulder. "Thank you, Axel. Truly."

He shrugs off my hand and glares at me. "That's the last fucking time I'm going to talk to you about love and my sister, alright?"

"I got you."

"Just note that if you do one thing out of line with her, I will whoop your ass into kingdom come, you got that? One fucking teardrop falls from her face on account of you and your behavior towards her, and you're *dead*."

"Received," I reply with a nervous laugh. "Loud and clear."

# 17

*CHLOE*

I'm TRYING to stomach some instant noodles and freaking the freak out about the meeting with the record producer tomorrow when there's a knock on the apartment door. It's just past midnight, so this surely isn't a delivery.

And I know it's not Gary because he told me he'll be out all night on a date. Plus, he has keys.

And it's not going to be Maddie.

*What the hell...*

I slowly lower my fork and cautiously tiptoe across Gary's living room towards the door.

*Who could possibly be knocking at the door at this hour?*

There's another knock.

There *is* somebody there.

And I do the only thing I can do.

"Who is it?"

There's a long pause before the person – *knockee?* – answers back.

"It's Bishop, Chloe. Open up."

*Oh, fuck.*

He can't be here. I've got the most important meeting of my life tomorrow. My entire musical future hangs on how I perform. I need to eat, shower, and then sleep so I'm ready for this nerve-wracking meeting. I cannot be dealing with this man yet again. Didn't I tell him to leave me alone forever?

He knocks again, the bastard.

*He's not going to stop, isn't he?*

I huff, exasperated, and open the front door, but just a little bit. Enough to see the man's very handsome face.

He's smiling, of course. Dimples forever. Reveling in the chaos he's brought here.

"Get lost, Bishop," I hiss through the crack.

The moment his name leaves my mouth, the rockstar pushes against the door – and in the process *me* – allowing him the space to simply step into Gary's apartment.

*Asshole.*

"Let's talk properly, Chloe," he snarls.

He confidently shuts the door behind himself as if to say that this is going to be a *long* talk. I have no intention of it being thus.

"You shouldn't be here," I bark at him, nodding help-fully towards the exit.

"I can be wherever I like. I want to talk to you again, Chloe. *See* your pretty face again."

"I want you to go."

But I do feel *something*. My words are sharp, but they come out of my mouth weak and pathetic. No conviction at all, and Bishop knows that.

This man has come here to hunt me down. He saw me that one time yesterday at my brother's place and it's like I've become his only thought since then. His goal. Every-thing he's doing is for me. To reclaim me like some prize.

And, admittingly, it turns me on.

It really shouldn't.

*But I really want him.*

"You can't speak to me like that," Bishop sneers under his breath.

I've lost my breath.

I feel my chest heaving. Bishop's eyes wander down to my breasts. I see the unfiltered lust behind that dark gaze.

All I need to do is utter one word and he'll take me right here, right now. This man hasn't gotten over me. He told me at the karaoke bar that I'm the one girl he wants. All the millions of girls that he could have at this moment, and yet he only wants me. Enough that he's come here at midnight to *talk*.

*Surely that's grounds to be turned on by, right?*

"You really have to go, Bishop..."

I don't get a chance to finish the sentence when Bishop takes me by the waist and pushes me against the back of the door, pinning my wrists above my head against the wall with his strong hands. I struggle with little effort.

To be honest, I'm completely turned on. My panties are soaked. There's a heat in the pit of my stomach. My nipples ache from being so hard.

I know I should feel afraid that this man has got me completely under his control, but I don't. I'm so driven by my horniness that I don't even mutter any more protests.

Bishop is a man who knows what he wants.

*Me.*

"Give in to your primal lust," he whispers, drawing his mouth a mere inch from my ear. "I know you want me, sweetheart."

I gasp.

"I don't want you."

"Sure, you do. Stop lying to yourself."

"Bishop..."

"You can't fight anymore, Chloe. I have you now. Exactly where I want you. Exactly where you want me. I could do whatever I wanted to you right now and you'll love it."

"And what would you do to me that'll make me love it?"

"Worship your body. Make you squeal my name. Make you feel like no man has ever made you feel."

"You really think you can do that, huh?"

"Just say the word and I'll make you mine."

And, at that moment, all my defenses fold. I can't resist him.

"I want you, Bishop. Do what you want to me."

He licks the side of my neck before he spins me around so that my face is up against the wall. His fingers quickly break through my wet panties and then he's inside me. His finger performs a *come hither* movement inside my warm pussy and my body rises and falls with his command.

And I love it.

My hips lift, and I find my sex succumbing to his power. My pussy shifts in reaction to the man. Obliging. Bending into submission. Bishop presses his front into my back. I feel his stiff erection up against my thigh.

*He wants me. He wants me so bad.*

"Bishop..."

"Be quiet and let me fuck you, princess."

I gulp as the rockstar drops my panties to my ankles. I've got no willpower to fight. No desire to even force him away.

*I want him. I want him so bad.*

I want to see what he does to me.

His manhood engulfs me from behind. My wet opening gives way and allows that thick wide shaft to enter.

*Oh, I remember Bishop like this all too well...*

This time, he's even more in control of us. Even more willing to let his primal lust overtake and consume us both. He's certainly not a boy anymore, and he demonstrates that with his deep, powerful thrusts inside me.

"You really should stop lying to yourself," Bishop murmurs into my ear, breathy from the all the explosive energy he's catapulting in my direction. "This is exactly what you've been after all this time, and you know it."

I nod and bite my lip. "Yeah, it is..."

I can't hide it any longer.

My cheeks flushing hot with desire, my face is violently pressed against the wall as Bishop has his way with me. His length is deep inside as his fingers continue to press. Between his thumb and index finger, he pinches my clit, making me squirm and yelp in exhilaration. He's so tall behind me. So in control. His hand cups my ass and squeezes me, stiffening my body against his cock.

There's a buzzing from deep inside me. Real-life physical pleasure mixed with a cavernous longing.

*This* is what I've been missing for so long. My body remembers this; how only Bishop can rock my core like this.

His rhythmic thrusting and teasing of my clit with his delicate guitar-playing hands brings me to the edge of a fiery orgasm.

"I'm going to finish," he barks, grunting in such a deep way.

"Yes."

My excitement builds as the rockstar thrusts even harder and faster.

"You want me. You need me, Chloe."

"I do..."

"Say my name."

"Bishop. Bishop. *Bishop*."

"You so want me... want me... want me..."

Him saying that truth over and over as he orgasms inside me, his lust for me no longer concealable, drives me insane. My legs tremble as I, too, reach climax. Bishop grunts one last time as I tilt my head back and cry out.

"*Bishop!*"

Everything's so hot. So high.

I've never felt more connected to anyone else. I've never felt so used. So *desired.*

Bishop's heavy breathing ceases.

Something doesn't seem right.

I turn to face him.

"You're going to wake up in a moment, Chloe, and you're going to realize this has all been a dream inside your head."

Bishop speaks flatly to me. I blink at him, not fully comprehending what he means.

"What?"

"This little encounter didn't happen. Hasn't happened. This is all your overactive imagination telling you exactly what you really want. You might try to deny me in real life, but you can't deny my hold over you. You want something like this to happen. You're *wishing* for it."

"This can't be a dream, Bishop. It felt so real."

He clicks his fingers at me.

"Time to wake up, Chloe."

* * *

"Good morning, Chloe. I've got coffee and a donut, so don't ever say I'm not a good host. Now give me that five-star rating on the app."

Gary bursts through my bedroom, waking me up from the sex dream.

*Yeah, it really was only a sex dream, wasn't it?*

Bishop didn't actually come around here last night. He didn't pursue me down. He didn't break in and push me against the wall. He didn't fuck me until I screamed his name.

I should feel relieved, but I really don't.

Dream Bishop was right. I'm wishing in my deepest core for that to have actually happened.

*Fuck.*

I cover my body with the bedsheets. Between my legs I am most definitely wet, and I don't want Gary to suspect a thing.

"Thanks," I mutter at him.

"Big day today," he says. "Good luck. I'll leave these on the bedside table."

He places the donut and takeaway coffee cup next to me and gives me a warm smile.

Yeah. The meeting today.

And all I've been thinking about is Bishop Hayes.

*Double fuck.*

"Thanks," I repeat.

Gary leaves the room, leaving horny-ass me behind. I should be focused on my music, not on some rockstar ex.

I can't get lost in my fantasies, especially if they're about Bishop.

I've got a job to do today.

# 18

CHLOE

THEY MAKE me wait for twenty minutes.

Twenty *freaking* minutes.

And the entire time I feel like I'm on the cusp of a heart attack. I sit there in the vast waiting room outside Mickey Miller's office and try to calm myself as my head explodes. I feel sweat building. I clasp my guitar. My foot taps against the carpet.

Above me, hanging on the high walls of this office, are black and white photos of all the famous bands and musicians Mickey Miller has produced. All frames signed with loving messages. People I have spent my entire life looking up to as inspiration, all produced by the one man I'm about to see. All glaring down at me as if to say...

*You're not worthy, Chloe Stoll.*

"He's ready for you."

It's the hot young blonde English receptionist. The one who signed me in and looked me up and down so dismissively when I approached her. Like I'd somehow managed to break in.

This entire building is designed to make people understand how much of a big player Mickey Miller is. It's designed – with its high ceilings and long-ass hallways and legendary artists' signatures and shining music award trophies on display - for lowly people like me to feel like I do not belong here.

This is the beating heart of the North American music industry.

"He is?"

The receptionist sighs. She's not going to repeat herself.

"Follow me."

I trail behind the hot receptionist with her scarily ice-cold English accent through the massive double doors at the end of the hallway and straight into Mickey Miller's sprawling personal office.

This room is even more impressive than the hallway outside. He's got gold records hanging around the walls. A whole trophy cabinet of awards he's personally won behind his long desk. There's a photo on his desk of a superyacht. I bet it's his. There's another photo of him shaking the President's hand. Another one of him with Paul McCartney.

And behind that impressive desk sits Mickey Miller himself. I recognize him immediately from the photos. If you can picture a stereotypical record producer, then Mickey Miller is *it*. A big man in his late sixties who knows every cent he's worth. Expensive suit. All veneers. Tanned skin. Botox. Clearly a hair transplant. Beady eyes that glare.

He's the full Hollywood music industry package.

And he's scary as hell.

He leans back in his chair and cups his hands together as if to pray as his receptionist introduces me in her cut-glass posh English inflection.

"Miss Chloe Stoll for you, sir."

The receptionist leaves, shutting the double doors behind her. Feels like she's locking me in with a monster.

I'm still on the other side of the room from Mickey Miller. About ten yards separate us. Ten yards across a chasm of an office.

Mickey Miller regards me with his small eyes. He doesn't make a sound. His expression is completely blank.

I have a very strong sense he doesn't know who the hell I am.

He probably hasn't even seen my viral video. Call it a hunch, but I don't think this is the guy who scrolls through Instagram all day.

*Have I made the biggest mistake of my life coming here? Am I about to be spit out?*

He doesn't invite me to take a seat or come any closer. I wonder if I should walk over and shake his hand.

But before I do, he finally speaks.

"Have you brought any songs with you?" he asks in a dull voice.

"Um... yep."

"Why the hesitation? I've heard you're a songwriter. Well, that's what you told my assistant. Show me some songs."

I nod. I know I've gotta act more confident. This is my chance. "Sure."

I reach into my bag and pick out my notepad.

And I immediately proceed to drop the damn thing on the fancy carpet like a clumsy idiot.

*Shit.*

I chuckle nervously before bending over and picking it back up. The producer just watches me without a word being spoken.

The silence is killing.

*Oh God.*

I carry the notebook over to him. He doesn't reach for it, instead, he motions – with just his eyes – to his desk. I leave it there. Eventually, he leans forward and, with the least amount of effort, flips through it.

I can't tell what he's thinking as he browses through an entire lifetime of songs. His eyes are reading, though. That should be good, right?

It's hard not to keep repeating in my head as Mickey reads through each page that this man's word has ultimate power in the music industry.

After skimming through a few more pages, he shuts the notebook.

"I saw your video," he says. "You are good at writing songs, Chloe Stoll, but you have no real experience. I want you to have some before you come back. Goodbye."

*That's it?*

He leans back in his chair with finality. Like that's the entire meeting over.

"I've been doing music for my entire life," I blabber out. "I've been making videos for seven years. I've flown all this way from my hometown because you asked to see me."

"My assistant asked to see you, not me. I didn't know who you were until ten minutes ago." I want to cry, but I hold back the tears. Other than him laughing me out, this is the worst way this meeting could've gone. And Mickey Miller isn't finished with me yet. "I've been in this business for thirty years. I don't go for wannabe musicians and definitely not for someone who simply has had a viral video. I'm looking for solid talent, not a flash in the pan. Maybe I should tell my assistant to be more discerning in future. Or I could fire her."

But I'm not leaving without a fight.

"Please reconsider," I say. "I've worked my ass off to be here right now."

Mickey regards me up and down. I feel like it's the first time he's properly looked at me since I've entered. I can see the thoughts turning in his head.

"Okay. Fine. *Sing*. Right now."

"Sing?"

"Yes, go ahead."

"Can I get my guitar..."

"Sing."

*Now?*

I open my mouth to sing, but no words come out. My whole body is tense with nerves. Sitting here, in his massive *fuck-off* office surrounded by trophies of all his glories, is not exactly the best environment to burst out a capella.

Mickey allows me a moment of songlessness before he simply sighs and gestures a finger back towards the double doors, guiding me to the exit.

No word spoken.

That really is it, then.

Meeting over.

\* \* \*

I can't recall leaving the office. I can't recall rushing down the hallway nearly in tears. Everything is just a blur of emotions. My heart is beating super fast.

*There are no two ways about it. I am a failure.*

Everything hinged on that meeting, and it totally, royally screwed up.

I don't even bother waiting for the elevator to take me downstairs; I just burst down the stairwell. Step by step by step. I need to keep moving before I collapse in on myself.

*I need to get out of this building.*

In the lobby, I head straight to the revolving doors that lead outside.

*I need to go home. I need to get the hell out of Los Angeles.*

It was a total mistake coming here. Delusions of grandeur. I should've listened to what my mind told me. Now it's back to Crystal River. Back to my old job and Karen and her cigarette breaks.

As I pass through the revolving doors, I'm so emotional and trying to clench back my tears that I accidentally run straight into someone.

"Sorry..."

I mutter my apologies as they grab me by the shoulder.

I look up.

"Bishop?"

He stands above me.

"How did your meeting go?" he asks.

What's he doing? Why is he in this building? I don't want him to see me like this.

"Did you follow me here?"

"You look upset, Chloe."

"That's because that meeting went utter shit," I reply.

And I storm right past him before he can see me cry.

# 19

SEVEN YEARS AGO

*CHLOE*

I'M QUEUING by the side of the makeshift stage in Crystal River High's gymnasium, and I think I'm dangerously close to having a full-on panic attack.

*Just breathe in and out, Chloe. It's just performing. You've done this so many times.*

Yeah. In front of my TV. Not in front of a crowd.

The gymnasium is packed full of fellow high school students. Drake is a popular guy. When people heard about him holding auditions for his new band, the entire place got filled up with eager people ready to watch their classmates fail.

And a lot have.

Take the guy on stage right now for example. I think his name is Damien. He's a year below me and we've never interacted before, but right now he's making a total embarrassment out of himself by trying to do some kind of stand up routine on stage. I guess, knowing he can't sing, he thinks he can joke his way into Drake's band. The thing is that, unfortunately and very clearly, he *ain't* funny.

And the crowd is laughing. At him.

It's not just the nerves of auditioning for Drake's new band in front of – *seemingly* – the entire school that's freaking me out, but also what the hell's going on between my brother and Bishop.

Axel stormed out of the house when I confessed to him about our relationship. I don't know what's gone on between the two of them, but both Axel and Bishop have completely cut contact with me over the last few days. In fact, they've both disappeared. Even Axel has either been out of the house when I'm there or has locked himself in his room. He's not spoken a word to me. I have not even seen a passing glimpse of him. And, worse of all, Bishop is not responding to any of my numerous text messages or calls.

Maybe I've really screwed things up.

Maybe my relationship with Bishop is truly over.

And that's the reason why I can't sleep. Or eat. Or live. Not without Bishop.

The last few days have been hell. But I'm here, aren't I? I'm pursuing my passion.

*I can still make this work.*

I was hoping to maybe see Bishop today. Maybe he's swung by to hear me sing. I was hoping to spot him in the crowd to cheer me on. But, as I wait by the stage, there's no sign of him anywhere.

I'm all alone to face the worst.

Damien finishes his "set". He's practically booed off stage. The crowd is undeniably vicious.

It should be my turn next.

I'm about to head up the stairs to the stage when I hear Drake speak through the loud system.

"We have a last minute request for an audition. I think I'll let him on stage. Bishop Hayes, everybody."

I freeze as I see Bishop emerge from the back of the gym. From the audience. It's the first time I've seen the man in days. He strolls down the aisle to cheers from the audience. His confident swagger making everyone root for him, of course. Bishop knows how to work a crowd.

He carries a guitar. I know he can play it. I've heard him. He's even quite good.

I spot his face as he gets closer. He's got a black eye, presumably from a fight with my brother. There's no other explanation. It's clearly a punch, and only my brother can land a punch on Bishop Hayes.

I want to talk to him, find out what's going on, why he's ghosted me, but Bishop just rushes up on stage before I even get the chance.

He steps up to the microphone so blasé. So easily. It's like he was born to be in front of people. The girls certainly know who he is. There's cheering and whoops already, and he hasn't even sung a note yet.

"I've Bishop Hayes," he says to the adoring crowd as he readies the guitar in his hands. "And I'll like to perform a song I've written myself."

And then he starts singing.

Within a few words, I recognize the song.

It isn't his.

It's my song.

The one I wrote for him.

*When I see you,*
*my heart stops beating*
*How can I live*
*when you're right there?*
*All of my fear flies away*
*when you come to me*
*And kiss my lips*

I can't believe it.

I mean, he is both good at singing and playing the guitar, but it's *my* song. Not his.

He reaches the end of my song, and the crowd goes wild. They love him. I stare out in disbelief. They think he's written the song.

But it was the song I was supposed to sing today...

And Bishop knows it.

*Is this all one form of sick joke? Is he twisting the knife in me for telling Axel about us?*

"You want to be a singer?" Drake asks once the audience has quietened down, his voice echoing around the gymnasium.

Bishop shakes his head. "I know you want to be the lead singer. I'm just happy to play guitar, that's my first love. That, and writing songs from the heart."

"Good man," Drake says. "I think I might have an offer for you. Come and see me afterwards."

Bishop waves to him and the crowd before he jumps off the stage on the other side. I don't even get the chance to intercept him before he's disappeared.

And then it's my turn. Truly, this time.

"Chloe Stoll, you're up."

Drake's voice unnerves me, but I continue up the stairs onto the stage.

What can I do now? Perform the same song that Bishop just claimed to be his?

There are lights in my eyes. Drake's fitted out the gymnasium with nearly everyone that I go to class with. People are watching. Lots and lots of people. My peers from high school.

Drake sits in the front row. His handsome face judging me.

I bet that Bishop is out there somewhere right now,

judging me as well. Laughing at me. The thief who took my heart from me.

It's like my entire world has come crashing down.

"I'm going to perform a song," I stutter into the microphone, feeling very exposed.

"Great," Drake says, waving at me. "Go ahead."

My hands lock around the guitar. My body goes rigid. I can't even get a word out.

I can't perform. I really can't. Not after what Bishop has done.

It's like he's stolen the words out of my mouth when he went up here and sang my song.

I don't even get a word out before I'm running off the stage, never to sing live ever again.

# 20

*CHLOE*

I'M down to my last dollar, I'm driving aimlessly around Los Angeles, and – *worse of all* – I'm crying my stupid little heart out on the freeway because my dreams have been utterly, totally shattered. *Nothing* can solve my problems. I'm truly at the lowest of the low here.

The producer's harsh words echo in my ear as I drive.

*I'm looking for solid talent, not a flash in the pan.*

"You're such a fool coming to LA thinking your fantasies will come true," I whisper to myself with both hands tightly clutching the steering wheel as I change lanes for the hell of it. What direction I'm going? I don't even know. I just need to drive, to escape this nightmare.

I decide to call Mom.

"Hello?"

Mom's smooth voice immediately calms me, and I begin to tell her everything. I tell her how I came to LA. How I saw Bishop again. How I really thought I might've had a chance with my dreams and everything as I walked into

Mickey Miller's office, but also how I was being so stupidly naïve. All those years wasted just sitting around in my bedroom writing silly songs and uploading them online for no one to see. I've spent seven years working as a cashier, watching my brother and his band become famous, whilst I threw away the best years of my life. For what?

For nothing.

"You did become viral," Mom replies. "Which means you're good, Chloe. Talented. A few million people can't be wrong."

I scoff. "I'll make no money going viral unless I can release more music. Better quality stuff. But sometimes people just want to see handsome young men sing, don't they?"

"Don't become bitter, Chloe."

"Bitter? I've just had the biggest producer in the music industry ask me to leave his office."

"Never forget your dreams, Chloe," Mom tells me calmly. "If your dreams are worth fighting for, then fight with everything that you've got. Trust me. I should've fought harder when I was your age for the things I wanted. I thought I found true love once, but then I let it go."

I wipe the tears from my cheeks. "You mean Dad?"

On the other end of the phone, Mom takes in a deep breath.

"I loved your dad, Chloe, but I'm talking about a time before him."

"Oh."

I would really like to know more about this story, but suddenly there's a new notification on my phone. Someone else is trying to call.

"Sorry, Mom," I say. "Someone's trying to ring me. I'll call you back."

"Okay."

I switch to the incoming call, and immediately Mickey Miller's deep voice dominates the car's speaker system.

"Chloe Stoll?"

"Uh... hello?"

"It's Mickey Miller here."

*I know who it is.*

"Yeah?"

*What the hell does he want with me?*

"The funniest thing just occurred to me when you left. Bishop Hayes, of all people, stormed right into my office. He says he can help your situation, and, despite my better judgment, I listened to his request. I want to see you again."

"Okay, like, right now?"

"Turn around wherever you are and get back here in the next ten minutes. I won't wait any longer than that."

And then he hangs up.

I pull over to the side of the highway and sit there in shock for a moment.

*What has Bishop done?*

But I heard what Mickey Miller said on the phone. This might be my last chance. And what did Mom just tell me? Fight for my dreams?

I've got ten minutes to get back to the office, so I better stop crying and move my sorry ass.

# 21

SEVEN YEARS AGO

*CHLOE*

Axel is the first person to find me. I'm sitting under a tree behind the gymnasium, away from the crowds. It's a spot I like to come to sometimes to get away from the rest of the school. Axel knows that.

He finds me crying. Instead of trying to talk to me or reassure me about what's just gone on inside that gym, he simply sits down next to me and wraps his arm around my shoulder. I lean against him for a moment.

A big brother and his little sister alone together.

"All my dreams are over," I say to Axel in a whisper. "I can't even sing in front of other people, and Bishop took my song. He's broken my heart, Axel."

My brother says nothing. He gently strokes the back of my shoulder.

I sigh. My sobbing decreases. It's good to touch my brother again. I thought I had completely ruined things when I told him about Bishop and me the other day.

"I saw Bishop's black eye," I continue. "I know it was you."

"Yeah," my brother replies. "It was me."

"At first, I didn't want you to hurt him, but now I think it's kinda good that you did. Is that fucked up? It sounds like it is."

"I don't know what to say."

"Don't say anything at all and keep hugging me."

We sit there for a long time until Axel decides to stand up.

"I'll get you something to dry your eyes," he says. "I'll be back."

"Okay. Thanks."

I watch him head towards the high school bathrooms. I lean back against the tree and close my eyes. My tears sting my cheeks.

"Chloe."

Bishop's voice startles me. I stand up and face the man. He's approached silently and now stands not even five yards away.

"You have a lot of nerve showing your face after what you just did in there," I say to the thief, barely able to contain my rage.

Bishop merely shrugs.

"I just wanted to let you know that I've just spoken to Drake. Axel was there as well. We're going to form this band with another guy in our year named Caspian. We're going to call ourselves Ravaged."

"I don't care," I reply, crossing my arms. "You stole my song."

"And you told Axel about us. He gave me this," Bishop says as he points to the vicious bruise covering his eye. It's even worse close up. "I told you not to tell him, but you went and did anyway, without any regard for my feelings. Stealing your song to get into Drake's band is simply my revenge."

"But why my song?"

"Maybe I just thought I'll be cooler for singing it, had you thought of that? Maybe I deserve to be in a band."

"You always said you didn't want to audition."

"Well, here we are."

"We're over," I seethe at him. "Forever. I never want to see you again."

Bishop scoffs. "I figured."

And it's at this moment when Axel reappears with a bag of tissues. He sees Bishop. He stops.

There's a wariness between the two best friends I've never seen before. They both stare each other down.

"Axel..."

I start, but Bishop doesn't let me finish. He jumps in, facing my brother.

"Chloe has just told me we're over, Axel. That's it. Done. You can stop hating me now and let's be members of this band with no animosity."

Bishop then smirks at me.

That's enough for me.

He's won. He's got his revenge. He's hurt me where it hurts.

*I lost.*

And I turn and walk away, crying once again. The tears are unrestrained now as I head off out of the school.

Axel doesn't follow me. I guess this new band is more important than his little sister.

My love life is ruined. Bishop has just mocked me in front of the entire school and my brother, and I just know that it's going to be a long fucking time before I can ever even think of performing in public again.

# 22

*BISHOP*

CHLOE WALKS through the door and the first thing she does is glare at me. If looks could kill, then I'd be dead. Her eyes drift from me to Mickey Miller. I'm standing next to the record producer sitting at his desk.

Her face betrays trepidation, anger... and a little bit of hope.

I'm glad she's come back. I honestly thought that her determination never to see me again would take priority over her music career.

After I saw her downstairs – when she ran into me and blurted out how bad the meeting went – I immediately made my way up here. I stormed past Mickey's protesting receptionist and burst into this room. I told Mickey Miller – the biggest fucking voice in the music industry - in no uncertain terms that he was making a big fucking mistake not even considering bringing Chloe on. He told me she choked up when he asked her to sing. I told him to give her another chance.

And he has.

And now she's here, and I don't dare speak. I leave all that to the producer next to me.

Mickey Miller and I go way back. To the very beginning of Ravaged. He was the first producer to see our potential. Signing on with him was the beginning of the boys and me becoming the stars we are today. Sure, we never saw much of the man. He's not exactly the type to come to recording studios and mingle with his stars, but he is the man with the power. All of the power, in fact. This man sitting next to me *is* the North American music scene.

And, like many hundreds before her, he has Chloe's entire future life in his hands.

Technically, he could even ruin mine as well for how I've burst into his office. Everyone, even the biggest stars on the planet, is terrified of this man. But I don't care. Not when I need him to give my girl a second chance.

"Chloe. Welcome back," Mickey Miller says in his flat drawl. "I'm going to give you another shot. Bishop has been quite persuasive that you're a better musician than I gave you credit for. That you ain't just a passing internet fad. So I'm going to organize for you to sing in front of my executive team in three days. We'll see then if you live up to what Bishop promises. Are you going to be ready for that?"

Chloe blinks. I can see that she is as nervous as hell. She slowly takes in the information. The last time I saw her as terrified as this was when she stepped up on stage in Crystal River High's gymnasium to audition for Ravaged.

"In front of your team?" she asks. "Live?"

"You're not going to choke up again?" Mr. Miller asks.

"Yeah, I might be ready," she blurts out.

Mickey Miller leans back in his chair with a groan. "I thought so. And I've also been thinking that I'll get Bishop to coach you over the next few days, seeing as he's so keen to vouch for you. You are his responsibility now."

Chloe's eyes dart back up to me accusatory.

I didn't know anything about this. Mickey and I didn't discuss anything about me coaching her. The producer sits there with a smug look on his face as both Chloe's and my faces drop.

Chloe goes from terror to disgust.

"What?" she asks. "Bishop is going to coach me?"

The producer grins for the first time all day, his fake teeth shining.

"Yes, he is."

# 23

*CHLOE*

Bᴉsʜop ɢʀᴀʙs my arm from behind as I walk out of the producer's office, clearly wanting to get my attention. I just knew he'd attempt something like this – forcing me to spend time with him, *coaching* me - hence why I've tried to leave this freaky building as fast as I can.

"Chloe…"

I spin around to face him. "What just went on in there?" I ask the rockstar both sharply and as quietly as possible so that neither Mickey Miller nor his receptionist can hear.

"Chloe."

He says my name again, and it's freaking infuriating. He leans in close to me, his lips forming into a sad pout. Is he trying to appear… *caring?*

That is certainly not one of Bishop's strong emotions.

I rip my arm away from his grip. I'm not having that.

"Don't give me such a dopey face," I say to him, rolling my eyes. He really wants me to think he cares? I don't know what game he's been playing with that record producer, but I don't like the feeling that I'm being humiliated somehow. They want me to play in front of a board of suits? And Bishop is supposed to coach me to do this? It all sounds like a practical joke and I'm at the receiving end.

You can't blame me for thinking that. Bishop has got a past form for embarrassing me in public.

*Screw him. I'm not losing my dignity to appease a producer, even if he's the biggest one in the world.*

"You heard what Mickey Miller said," Bishop tells me. "He's actually giving you a second chance."

"Is that what you call it? Sounds a lot like he wants me to entertain his high-flying friends. *Here, look at this poor nervous girl who can't get a word out.*"

Bishop stands back. He's frustrated with me, but he's deciding to hide it. "This is another chance, Chloe. A lot of people don't get something like this."

"And you want me to thank you for it? My savior?"

"Chloe, it's Mickey's idea that I coach you for this thing. I never asked to do it."

"Bullshit. You love that we're now paired up."

"I'm telling the truth. I didn't know about it until just then when he told you."

"Well, I'm sure you can forgive me for not believing you after your past record."

"Whatever you believe, you just simply have to take this second offer up," he says. "It's too good to turn down. This is your big shot, your last big shot, and I can help."

"I don't need you to help me, Bishop. I don't need you to help me practice. In fact, I don't *need* you at all. The past seven years are testament to that fact."

"But you still choke up when you perform, don't you?"

*Really. Screw him.*

"I'm refusing to talk about this. None of this concerns

you. I know that this is a good opportunity for me, and that's why I'm going to do this on my own."

I spin back around to walk away, but Bishop's voice follows me.

"Mickey Miller won't see you again unless you practice with me."

*God damnit.*

He's right.

That's what the producer said. I've just been trying to live in denial. If I'm going to have a second chance at this, then the truth is that I'm going to have to deal with Bishop Hayes.

The very last man I want to work with.

I stop dead in my tracks, resigned to the fact that I'm going to have to talk to the man who broke my heart. Get freaking *coached* by him.

"Do you really want this, Chloe?"

I turn back around to the rockstar. He's leaning against the wall like he's in some goddamn photoshoot. And, yeah, he looks hot. He always looks so damn hot.

His intense stare with those deep brown eyes of his bores straight through me. I feel a shudder pass down my spine as he waits for my answer. It's like I'm his entire world. Like I'm the most important thing in existence right now. His desire for me permeates the air between us, and I feel my breath leave my body.

I really do want this opportunity so bad. This is why I've flown all this way to a city I hate and am considering working with a man I want nothing to do with. Simply to do what I feel like I was born to do.

"I'll give you one lesson," I say. "One. That's it. Screw it up and I'm really never seeing your ass again."

The faintest of smiles crosses the rockstar's face.

"Well then," he says. "Come to my place tonight."

## 24

*BISHOP*

I open my front door and, just on cue, there's Chloe Stoll giving me the death stare I've come to get quite familiar with these last few days. She's holding her guitar case with both hands like it's a shield between us.

"Let's get this over with," she grumbles as she steps inside my place.

"You're still showing me hostility, then?" I ask her snidely as she just walks on into my home without any regard for an invitation or even a guided tour. She powers on down towards the living room with me following close behind. She's really trying to give off the vibe that she does not, in any way, want to be here with me.

*Well, I do like a challenge.*

"Things don't get forgotten simply because you can sweet talk a producer into giving me another shot, Bishop," she mutters back to me as she strolls on through. "That's why there might still be a *little* bit of hostility from me."

I shrug. "Fair enough."

"This place is huge," Chloe remarks once we reach my living room. "This is where you live? On your own?"

I follow her gaze around the room. Yeah, it is pretty big, but I've never really thought about it before. I don't care much about interior design or anything. I simply had Lucas find me three houses in LA. I had a look around each one, and this place seemed pretty cool, and then I hired some famous designer guy to do his thing. And *voila*.

But it all seems to have impressed Chloe. That makes me smile.

"I just have so much money to throw away," I reply. "I've got so much I don't know what to do with it, and I needed a place to base myself. So this is where I live."

Chloe wanders up to the grand piano in the corner of the living room. Now, that is an expensive piece of equipment, even for me. I had it personally made and shipped from Europe. Some Austrian company that's been making pianos for hundreds of years did it for me.

"Holy shit," Chloe says as she plays a few chords and admires the sound it makes. "You really do have a lot to throw away."

She turns her attention to the kitchen, marveling at it.

"I don't cook," I say. "I usually just get delivery."

"But you could cater for an entire restaurant in here."

"It came with the house. On tour, we have our own private chef."

Chloe scoffs at me. "You're crazy. Ravaged's success has gone to your head."

"Has it, really?" I ask her, dead seriously. "I'm still pining for the same girl I knew in high school."

She rolls her eyes at that and continues through outside where my pool is. It's a long one that lights up at night.

"What are you doing with such a massive pool?" Chloe asks me, dipping her toe in the warm water.

"I like to swim in it," I reply, deadpan.

She laughs and wanders back inside. I follow her to the couch.

"But do you miss Crystal River?" she asks as we sit opposite each other. I'm glad she's starting to open up and is no longer swearing at me to leave. Who knew that my house would be such an ice-breaker?

I shrug at her question. "Yeah, I do. I've actually been thinking of moving back. I don't need Los Angeles anymore. I'm in the biggest band on the planet, so I can live anywhere I want and just get a private jet to wherever I need to be."

"Are you serious?"

"I'm not much of a city boy."

"No, I was talking about the private jet."

"Oh, yeah. Well, of course we have a private jet. I *am* a rockstar, Chloe."

"This is a whole other world," she says, eyes wide. I think she's finally coming to terms with how crazy my life has become since we last met.

But, despite all the money and success, some things never change. Your feelings for someone. Your heart.

*Fucking hell, listen to me. I've gone soft.*

Maybe some of my band's love lyrics have gone to my head. I've been completely blindsided since seeing this girl again. It's like my whole world's gone upside down. I've finally woken up to how much I need her back again in my life.

*Yeah, some things really never do change.*

"Alright, I guess it's time for you to show me some songs," I say.

"What?"

"I know you've written a lot of songs, Chloe."

"I don't show people my works in progress."

"Good thing I'm not like other people, then," I reply.

140

"Plus, this is important. It'll be a smart move at this performance to do original songs. Those executives will like that."

"Fine," she says. She pulls out a notebook from her guitar case. It's clearly seen some work. The ends are battered, and it's definitely been opened a whole lot of times. I bet Chloe takes this book everywhere. She reluctantly hands it over to me.

"Are there any songs about me?" I ask her with a smirk.

"Only the shit ones."

I start to browse through. Chloe's neat handwriting is scribbled all over the pages. So many songs. I read through a few.

"These are good," I say, and I'm telling the truth. They *are* good. She has a way with writing and it has definitely improved a billion times since we were teenagers.

"I just write all the time," Chloe says. "I have to get the words out, otherwise I'll go crazy. Well, more crazy than I am usually."

I turn the page and read another.

*It's only you I think of*
*You who made my world spin*
*I want you to come back*
*And tell me you're sorry*
*Sorry for everything*

"THIS SONG'S DEFINITELY ABOUT ME," I say, pointing it out to her.

"Um..."

She can't find an excuse fast enough.

"You want me to apologize?" I ask. "For what?"

"For what you did," Chloe says.

"There's nothing to apologize for."

Chloe shakes her head and stands up. "I'm leaving," she exclaims, grabbing the notepad out of my hand. "I knew coming here was a mistake."

"You're risking your music career because I won't say the word *sorry*?" I ask her.

"I am."

"I don't understand you, Chloe."

"Self-respect is more important than anything."

"Well, I ain't saying it."

"And that's why I'm leaving," she retorts.

And she actually does. She walks straight out of my house.

"Fuck me," I say under my breath as she slams the front door. "Fucking *women*."

## 25

*CHLOE*

SCREW BISHOP.

And screw his non-apology. And that smug look he gave me in defiance.

I walk straight out of his place and don't stop. I sprint, holding my guitar case in both my hands, towards the nearest bus stop. I'll get a bus back to Gary's and never come back.

I hate being like this. Having to do this. But I have too much respect for myself. I'm not going to hang around a guy who isn't prepared to even acknowledge the pain in the past between us. Who openly looks at me in surprise when I even mention that he once hurt me.

Bishop says that I'm jeopardizing my career because I want him to apologize for the way he treated me? Well, if that's the case, then maybe I should just get on the next flight home.

And I should. Los Angeles is not where I want to be. It's

all over. I shouldn't have even entertained the thought of Bishop coaching me. It's impossible.

On the other side of the road, I see my bus pull up at the stop. I yell out for it to wait and dart across the road, but my foot hits the curb and I go flying.

And so does my precious guitar.

As I tumble to the road, I watch the guitar in absolute terror as it flips out of the case and straight below the wheels of a passing truck. I wasn't thinking when I left Bishop's place. I didn't lock the case properly.

And now I stare from the ground as the guitar I've had practically all my life gets completely destroyed right in front of me under a speeding vehicle.

*No, no, no, no.*

# 26

*CHLOE*

"And, for the second time in one day, everything in my life went to complete crap," I say as I stab my carrot, ginger, and apple juice with a paper straw.

"Well, you've stuck it out this far," Gary replies, sighing. "Maybe you should keep going."

I scoff. "How can I keep going when I have no guitar?" I ask.

Gary raises his own straw up to his lips. "That's true."

It's the morning after the whole failed Bishop practice. When I woke up this morning and told Gary about what happened yesterday, what with the first crazy meeting with Mickey Miller, then whatever the hell went on with Bishop, and then when the truck ran over my beloved guitar, my host decided to buy us takeaway juices and to sit down and talk about it in his living room.

"Can anything get worse than this?" I ask the man. "I have nothing left. No guitar. No career..."

"Why don't you ask your brother for money if you're so broke you can't afford a guitar?" Gary suggests.

"Because I'm very stupidly boneheaded about something like that. I've got too much of a.. thing to beg my famous brother for money. I made a secret promise to myself when Ravaged took off that I wouldn't rely on him for anything."

"Ah, right," Gary replies. "Very noble of you, even if it is yourself kicking yourself in the butt."

"Well, there's nothing I can do now," I sigh. "As I've said, it's all gone to crap."

"Oh, Chloe..."

"Thank you for letting me stay, though. You've got a really lovely place, and you've been one source of light in a city like Los Angeles, so thank you again, Gary."

"What are you talking about? Having you here has been an absolute joy. I've met a real-life famous person."

"Two, technically. If you count Bishop."

"I'm not counting that man."

I smile. "Thanks, Gary. You're the best. I've got to pack up and go home now. I'm so sorry for having messed you around."

"Don't be sorry at all," Gary says. "We better stay friends, girl. I can't believe I've had someone to stay who is as goddamn funny, smart, and talented as you."

I smile at him before I drink the rest of my juice and head to my room to pack. Now that my guitar is completely smashed, there isn't much for me to actually put away.

As I pack my things into my bag, there's a loud knock on the door. Someone really wants to be let in. I hear Gary's muffled voice saying he'll get it.

A moment later, I hear raised voices. Gary arguing with someone.

I poke my head out of the doorframe to check who it is, hoping in the pit of my stomach it isn't the man I think it is.

*Nope. I'm right.*

There's Bishop.

Because of his extreme height, my ex is standing over Gary, practically leaning over him. But my host is not letting their height differences affect him in any way; he's got a threatening finger poking in the direction of Bishop's face.

"She's leaving now, you know."

"I want to see her," Bishop replies quietly. He hasn't noticed me peeking around the corner.

"After the way you've treated her? Not likely."

*Wow, go on Gary. You go, girl.*

Bishop stares him down in disbelief. He doesn't get talked to like this much, that's for sure. "What would you know?"

"I know enough for you to get the hell out of my house."

"It's okay, Gary," I finally speak up. "I'll talk to him. For a moment."

Both their faces turn in my direction. Gary looks at me in concern. Bishop looks at me like a man in the desert looking at water.

"I'll give you a minute," Gary says, resigned. "But I'll be in my room if you need me, Chloe."

He flashes a warning look at Bishop as he passes the man.

I step into Gary's living room and cross my arms at Bishop.

"Go on," I request him sternly. "Tell me why you're here. It better be good, or I'm shutting that door on your face."

# 27

*CHLOE*

"So, this is the gay guy's place, then?" Bishop asks as he strolls into the living room and glances around.

"It's *Gary's* place, yeah," I reply with a sigh. "So don't touch anything."

Bishop raises his hands in mock surrender. "I wasn't going to."

"Good," I say. I'm not going to offer him a seat. He's not going to be here for long. I just want to know why he's come all this way. It really better be freaking good. "You're not here to apologize, are you?"

"No."

"Great."

*He can leave now.*

"It's not why I'm here. But before you should say anything with that pretty mouth of yours, I've got something to give you."

I'm taken aback. "Me?"

He retreats back out the front door and returns a

moment later holding a black guitar case. Bishop offers it to me.

Oh. *Wow*.

"It's for you, Chloe."

I shake my head. "I can't take this, Bishop."

"Axel told me what happened last night with your guitar. I know I can't make up for how special that other one was to you, but this is still better than having nothing. I can't bear to think of Chloe Stoll without a guitar by her side. I can't even imagine that."

"My brother told you?"

"Well, technically Maddie told him and then he told me."

I shake my head again and refuse to reach out for it. "It's very kind, Bishop, but I don't want to accept any form of charity."

"Why would you think it's charity?" Bishop asks. "The guitar is not for free. I'm only giving it to you in return for payment."

"What kind of payment? I don't have money."

"You coming to continue your practice sessions with me," Bishop replies. He nods towards the case and I reluctantly take it from him. I place it on the ground and open it up, pretty damn curious to see inside.

It's a Gibson, exactly the kind of guitar that I've always wanted. The same kind I told Bishop I've always wanted years ago when we were playing that questions game in my bed.

There's a pang in my heart. He remembers.

*And it's so beautiful.*

A moan of approval escapes my lips as I bend down to inspect it even more. I don't care that I'm supposed to be refusing this gift. It really is exactly what I've desired but could never afford. My fingers trace along the curves of the gorgeous thing, admiring it.

"It's the one I told you about," I whisper.

"I've not forgotten a single thing about you, Chloe."

I look up at Bishop then. He's standing over me with the biggest smile on his face.

And a sudden realization crosses my mind.

*He wants me to be happy.*

"Bishop, it's too much..."

"You can pay me back by coming back to my place to practice. You can pay me back by doing this stupid performance and becoming the famous musician I know you should be. What do you say?"

I glance behind the rockstar into Gary's room. He's got the door open and he's standing there, peeking in at us. Gary encouragingly nods at me. I nod back.

"Fine," I say to Bishop Hayes. "You've got me. Let's go for another practice session."

# 28

*CHLOE*

I CAN'T GET over how nice it is to play this beautiful guitar. I find myself stroking it as I look up at Bishop.

"Why are you being so kind?" I ask him. "Buying me the guitar and everything?"

For the briefest of moments, it seems like he blushes. His cheeks go pink and he breaks eye contact with me. But that's the most I get to seeing behind the curtain before he's back to his cool self again.

We're back at his place, just like Bishop wanted. A few hours into practicing for the upcoming meeting with Mickey Miller and his team. Somehow Bishop has lowered my antagonism towards him and has actually got me performing some of my original songs.

It feels like we're living a memory. It's us again, as teenagers, back in my bedroom playing around.

*Oh, how I wish we could reverse the clock and go back to those happy days when there were no cares in the world and we snuck around in secret from my brother.*

"I saw you the other night at that karaoke bar," Bishop replies to me. "You were real good, just as I remembered. You've put in the work, I can tell. If there's anyone who deserves a new guitar, it would be you."

I roll my eyes at his compliment. I can't take any praises from him, not after the whirlwind of the last few days. This man can make me go from hatred at the sight of his face to sex dreams back to hatred again in a matter of hours.

*How can I even think about this performance when Bishop Hayes is dominating my thoughts?*

"You're really not going to apologize for what happened in high school, aren't you?" I ask him.

Yeah, I'm still hung up over that. But it's because it was such a big thing for us, and Bishop appears totally nonplussed about it as if I'm the crazy one to care.

He shrugs at my question. "If I didn't do what I did, then I wouldn't be here in this position," he replies. "In this house."

"Wow."

It's all I can say in response.

"You told Axel about us, remember? Even when I asked you not to, you went ahead and told your brother. I was a teenage boy who wanted retaliation, and I got it."

"And that was wrong of me, but also so wrong of you to... *retaliate.*"

"How about we just don't talk about it and focus instead on getting a good performance out of you," Bishop replies quietly. "I want you to do well. I've *always* wanted you to do well."

I can't stay mad for long. Not when he looks at me like this. His intensity makes me want to blush.

My gaze travels to his lips. Those same lips that used to kiss mine. I miss those long nights in my bedroom when I would wait up for him, bristling with excitement, just to hear my window open and him climb through. The first thing he would do every time was kiss me. I've wanted that for a long time.

Maybe I should just let the past be the past. If there's anything these last few crazy days have taught me if that I not only miss our kisses, but I also miss *him*. I've never felt as safe or as loved as when I did in his arms.

The guitar hangs loose between my arms as Bishop and I fall into a moment of silence. We're both staring at each other.

"I wish we could just go back in time and stay at the moment when I showed you the song I wrote for you," I say, breathless.

Bishop doesn't even break eye contact this time. He seems completely unfazed by my wish. Like he was expecting it. "I wish so too," he says.

My skin tingles like goosebumps.

"It was my favorite moment."

"It was my favorite moment, too."

And now, despite my better judgment, I wish he would kiss me.

I know he senses the moment too.

But instead of doing what I want him to do, Bishop just calmly stands up and walks over to his surround music system. He's teasing me. He's not ready to kiss me just yet.

*But what's he waiting for?*

He puts on an upbeat song and spins back around to me, the goofiest smile on his face.

"What are you doing?" I ask him.

"What does it look like?"

He starts to throw some shapes. Really corny moves that make me laugh.

"You're... *dancing?*"

"Come on," Bishop says, reaching out and taking my arm. "Dance with me."

"Okay..."

And he pulls me off the couch. And I'm dancing with him.

Bishop doesn't give a damn about what he looks like or how funny he looks trying to dance. So much so that it rubs off on me. I'm now dancing like him, wild and free.

He takes me by the hand and pulls me in close. His lips go to my ear and he's whispering.

"Remember when we used to dance together in your room? Back when there were CDs?"

I laugh again. His hands wrap around my waist and brings our bodies together.

I've forgotten how much damn fun Bishop is. He knows how to make me laugh. He knows how to make me swoon.

His eyes are all over my body, and I like it.

He takes me by the hand and spins me on the spot. I giggle. And then he tugs me in close again, and I start to dance slowly. *Seductively*. I want him to see what he's missing. I want to make him want me even more.

I want to tease him.

This is not a normal practice session, that's for sure, and I don't care.

# 29

*BISHOP*

I'm NOT LYING when I say that Chloe is really fucking good. Like international rockstar good.

And I should know.

When Mickey turned to me in his office and said that I was to coach her for the performance, I was very skeptical. I saw the look in Chloe's eyes. I knew there was a very low chance she would let me within ten yards of her. But she did. And - with a hell of a lot of encouragement on my end - she's slowly beginning to open up to me.

I'm prepared to do whatever it takes.

Even awkward dance moves.

But her performance with the famous producer and his executive team is tomorrow. We have just one more session to get this right.

*One more session with the girl I love.*

Dancing with her yesterday made me realize that I don't want these days to end. I want to stay with this girl. Forever.

*Fucking hell.*

That's such a weird-ass thing for a rockstar who's had every girl in the world froth at the mouth for me, isn't it? I should be spoiled for choice and have no need for this girl from my small hometown. But it's the truth. I don't care about any other pussy. I just want Chloe Stoll back in my life. Permanently.

For today's practice session, and last before her performance tomorrow, we're at her place. Or, rather, the apartment of that weird guy she's staying with.

*Yeah, I'm jealous of a gay man.*

"That was amazing," I say to Chloe as she finishes playing a song on her new guitar I have not heard yet. "Really fucking good."

*How many times can I repeat that?*

But she needs to hear all the praise she can hear, especially when it's the truth.

We're in her bedroom. Neither of us has admitted it, but we're both having flashbacks to her bedroom seven years ago. All those nights I spent chasing down the neighborhood just to climb through her window. The nights we spent staying up until the birds heralded the dawn, just holding each other and talking. Making plans. Revealing our deepest secrets.

*Where have those nights gone?*

All I've ever hoped for is for them.

And that's why this girl sitting on her bed next to me is the most important girl in the world.

"Thanks," Chloe replies. "Wait, are you crying, Bishop?"

"I'm not," I say.

But I am. I pretend to scratch my cheek whilst I subtly wipe a tear away. I don't know why I'm crying. I never cry. But something about Chloe's music... seeing her like this...

"Are you okay?" she asks me.

"Look, Chloe, you've done all this on your own, right? You've been getting ready for this for seven years on your own. Without a band around you. Not even using your brother's name to get views or be seen. It's great."

"That's probably because I'm *cooler* than you."

And then she knocks back her head and laughs. She's been wanting to rebuke me with that line for a long time, I can tell.

She is insane, but I love that.

"Are you ready, though?" I ask her.

Chloe shrugs, then her eyes glance downward. "Can you be at the performance tomorrow? For support?"

The fact that she's asking me that question makes me want to cry again.

"Chloe, I'm definitely going to be there."

"Thank you."

"What's wrong?" I ask her. "I know that face you're pulling."

"I'm worried about choking up in front of everyone," she says softly.

"You won't. You know the words and the songs inside out. They're *your* songs, written about *your* life. This is your soul you're revealing to Mickey Miller and his team tomorrow, and there's nothing wrong with that."

Chloe nods. "Okay."

"You alright?"

"Thank you for those nice words. It's been... good having you around these last few days."

Finally, a spark of something.

*I can work with this.*

I lean over and take her guitar from out of her hands. I gently lower it on her bed.

"I can see that you're nervous, so how about we stop

practicing and go for a nice dinner?" I ask her. "Together. My treat."

Chloe nods. "I'd like that very much, Bishop."

# 30

*BISHOP*

Harold, the most reviled paparazzi "journalist" in the world, is waiting outside the restaurant when we pull up in my car.

"This is my lucky day," the greasy-haired vulture says when I open the passenger door for Chloe, trying to ignore the man with all my willpower. "I sit outside this place all freaking day hoping to get some Z-list celebrity to snap and instead a member of Ravaged turns up. With a girl, no less."

As I take Chloe's hand to help her out, I finally give in. I face the so-called journalist and roll my eyes. "Get lost, Harold."

He snorts derisively, like a pig. "Never, Mister Bishop Hayes. Photos of Ravaged sell, and I've got to make a buck."

I guide Chloe with my hand around the front of the vehicle towards the entrance of the restaurant. Harold doesn't budge to let us pass him, the asshole.

"Haven't you made enough bucks from being such a creep?" I ask him as I brush past.

He chuckles. "Oh, you're such a tough guy. You think you're so cool, Bishop?"

"What you're doing is not honest work," I reply as I hand my keys to the valet. "It's gutter journalism."

"Whatever you say," Harold sneers back before he raises his goddamn camera and starts flashing in my face. "It sure pays the bills. I'll do anything for the perfect snap."

*If I weren't so civilized, I would be exchanging more than words with this rat.*

But then people on the street start to recognize me. Someone calls my name, and soon we're surrounded by people wanting a selfie with me.

"See," I say to Harold as his camera view is blocked by passersbys. "These are the people I actually want to take photos with. *Fans.*"

Harold grumbles and slumps away. His photos of me were probably blurred and unusable. Good.

I take my time and pose for photos with the fans. People are really sweet. I chat back to them, asking them what Ravaged songs they like the most. Meeting fans like this, even at an inconvenient time, is the reason I truly love this job. This is what matters. The music and the fans. Not the shit side of fame and gutter journalists.

I spot Chloe behind the crowd. She's standing there, watching me, with a smirk on her face.

I grin back.

She's getting to see what my life is like up close.

But more and more people join. I don't have the chance to see everyone unless I'm out here all night.

Restaurant security arrives and manages to sneak Chloe and me inside.

"Lucky we had you boys," I tell them. "Otherwise I would've been stuck out there."

"I bet you really enjoyed being the center of attention," Chloe whispers to me, nudging me in the ribs.

"Hey, I didn't become a sexy rockstar for nothing," I tell her.

The maître-D immediately recognizes me.

"Ah, hello, Mr. Hayes."

"Evening. Sorry, I haven't booked a table. Last minute thing, you know."

"I'm sure we can arrange something for you," he says.

Chloe lifts her head over his shoulder. "The place looks really busy, though," she remarks.

"Fully booked out, ma'am, but we'll find a table for such a star."

We're whisked off to a table in no time. I make sure to tip the maître-D on the way.

"You must really like being called a star," Chloe says to me as we sit.

"I'm actually very annoyed you don't call me one," I tell her.

She huffs, but I see that smile. I like making her laugh.

We order a whole table of really nice food. Lobster and caviar.

"I've never tried caviar," Chloe tells me.

"Like I said, it's my treat."

As we wait for our food, I pull out my phone.

"Sorry, I just have to do this," I excuse.

"What are you doing?" Chloe asks as I start typing.

"I'm sending an email to Mickey Miller to say we've been practicing and that I think you're totally ready for tomorrow. A full recommendation."

"You don't have to do that, Bishop."

"I know. I want to, though."

The food comes and we tuck in.

"Are you going to be there tomorrow?" she asks me.

I laugh. "You keep saying that. Of course, I'll definitely be there, Chloe."

"This restaurant is a lot different from anything you'll find in Crystal River."

I raise the glass of wine to my lips. "Yep."

Chloe gestures around the room. "Did you ever think any of this was going to happen to you when you started with Ravaged? Truly?"

I think about it for a moment. "No," I say. "Not in my wildest dreams. When Ravaged started, I didn't even think I would see you again."

Chloe looks down at her own glass of wine. "Do you see now that maybe what you did to me seven years ago was wrong?" she quietly questions. "That you should at least apologize?"

I lean back in my chair. This is a conversation I've been afraid of having. I really don't think what happened was that bad. Besides, she humiliated me by telling my best friend and her brother about our relationship, so I exacted my revenge.

*But that was all seven years ago. Why can't she forget it?*

"It was all the actions of a stupid teenager," I say. "But I'm not going to apologize for feeling what I did and doing what I did. I felt angry and needed to do something back to you. Sure, it was an idiotic thing to have done, but the past is the past, right?"

Chloe shakes her head. "Bishop..."

I lean forward and take her hand. "I love you, Chloe Stoll. I've always loved you."

There is not one lie in those words. It's what I feel. What I *know* I feel.

She seems to be accepting of that, and she's about to say something – her mouth opens and closes – but then she pulls her hand back.

And it's like all the affection she has for me disappears in that one moment.

"If you truly loved me, then why did you betray me?" she asks curtly. "In such a public way as singing one of my songs and pretending it was one of yours?"

I shrug. "There's nothing I can say. It happened."

"You're just going to sit there and shrug?"

"Yeah. Like I said, there's nothing to say."

Chloe shakes her head again and stands up.

"I'm not going to deal with this," she announces.

"What are you doing?"

"You can't even acknowledge the past," she whispers sharply. "You can't acknowledge my broken heart."

And then she walks away.

*So goddamn stubborn.*

"Chloe..."

I call out her name, but she doesn't answer.

She's still mad at me. And I know she's never going to forgive me.

Maybe this is it.

All our encounters seem to end with an argument. We can't seem to reconcile the past.

Maybe things between us will never work.

*You get crazy when I say goodbye*
*But I wouldn't have it any other way*
*You say those words, and I don't speak*
*And we tumble away*
*Oh, we tumble away*

# 31

*BISHOP*

I DON'T USUALLY REMEMBER my dreams, but tonight I do.

I'm at an airport, searching for something.

Someone.

Chloe Stoll.

She's getting on a plane, and I can see her even though she's at the other end of the terminal. I start running towards her, screaming her name.

But she doesn't see me. She doesn't hear me.

She's getting on the plane.

And then it starts to head down the runway.

And I'm following. I'm chasing the plane as it gears up, ready for takeoff.

I know I'll never see her again if the plane gets in the air, so I run and I run.

But I never catch it.

And I wake up sweating. I sit up in my bed and look down at my hands which are covered in my sweat. My breathing is heavy. It's like I'm having a panic attack.

As the fog clears from my head, a clear thought emerges.

*I don't want Chloe Stoll to go.*

# 32

*CHLOE*

Bishop doesn't message me all night. I stay up late, very late, waiting for something – *anything* – from him, even though I know I really shouldn't be doing this considering I have this crazy important performance today, but still... nothing comes.

*Nada*. Not a thing.

My alarm wakes me up, and I check my phone again.

Still no message.

I sigh and start to get ready for the performance today. I have a long hot shower because I can't be assed to step back out in the cold. I stand there with the water running over me, deep in thought over what happened last night between Bishop and me.

Yet again I walked away. How couldn't I, though? Yes, I felt like a kid throwing a tantrum in the middle of that restaurant storming off, but the way he simply brushed the past off like it was nothing just really... peed me off.

But he told me he loved me.

*Wow, your head is in shambles, Chloe.*

Even though I berate myself for thinking way too much about the man, the first thing I do when I leave the shower is to check my phone again for any messages from him.

I'm definitely caught hook, line, and sinker.

*Freaking hell.*

I'm angry at him. Angry about everything. But he *has* been so nice to me. The new guitar he got me. The cheesy dancing in his living room. The care he's shown me. The effort to prove he's a changed man. He's so different from my memories.

Maybe people do change.

*Ugh. Stop thinking about him, Chloe. Focus on the performance.*

I don't plan to eat breakfast; I'm just too damn nervous about today. I do eventually manage to make myself just some butter on toast to chew down, but then my phone rings, making me jump.

I nearly choke on the toast in my mouth as I scramble for my device, hoping – *praying* – that it's Bishop wanting to make amends for last night.

But it's not Bishop. It's my brother.

"Good luck with today, sis."

"Thanks, Axel."

"I hope it goes well for you," he says, in a rare moment of sincerity from him. "You deserve it. You've always been so persistent and focused on your goal of making it here. You've earned everything that's coming to you."

"Thanks."

"You really have, though. I love you, little sis."

I think I want to cry.

"I love you too, big bro."

It's weird for him to be so earnestly encouraging when our entire relationship is founded on our near-constant ribbing.

"There *is* something I need to say, Chloe."

I put my piece of toast down.

"Uh, oh. This doesn't sound good."

"No, it's nothing. Although it is a bit weird for a brother, especially one like me to be saying this, but I want to remind you that I chose to forgive Bishop."

"What are you saying?"

"What happened between him and me... it could have ruined things. It could have ruined Ravaged before it even began, but I chose not to allow it to. You understand? I forgave him for... sleeping around with my sister behind my back. And it was hard, but it needed to be done."

"Axel..."

"Please listen, Chloe. I want to tell you this. I know his actions towards you were worse, but sometimes you have to forgive so you can move on. Stop punishing yourself, Chloe. Don't let the love of your life go because of some grudge from seven years ago. I can see that you're hung up on it. On him. But life's too short to spend your best years hating on someone you love for a stupid mistake they once made."

"Has Bishop put you up for this?" I ask my brother sternly.

"No. He doesn't know a thing. He'll never want me talking to you like this, and I gotta admit it's awkward as hell for me. But Chloe, Bishop loves you. You know that, right?"

I close my eyes. "I do know," I reply softly.

*He told me last night.*

"You wouldn't be so angry with him if you didn't care so much," my brother adds. "God, you are as stubborn as I am, aren't you?"

*He knows me too freaking well.*

I say my goodbyes and hang up the phone before sitting down and letting out my second sigh of the morning.

*Damn it, Axel.*

I know it, even if I hate the truth. My brother is right.

# 33

*CHLOE*

I AM STANDING in front of Mickey Miller and a room full of his top executives...

And I'm choking up.

Just as I predicted I would, I cannot perform. Words can't escape my lips. My hands shake as I apprehensively grip my guitar against my chest.

I'm in the boardroom at the bigshot producer's office. They've made one side of the room into a makeshift stage, pushing back the boardroom table to give me space to stand in front of twenty or so of Mickey Miller's executives and the man himself in the front row.

*Oh God.*

But they shouldn't have bothered doing a thing.

Because I can't play a single note.

And they're all looking at me.

Judging me.

Just as it happened seven years ago in front of the entire school.

*No, no, no.*

My eyes dart for Bishop somewhere in the room, hoping he's there to offer me support. But he isn't there.

*I pushed him away last night. I've brought all this on myself. I ruin everything.*

This entire scenario is a nightmare come to real life. This time I ain't dreaming.

And so I do what I always do...

I run away.

*Coward. Coward. Coward.*

There are gasps as I step down off the stage in front of the assembled crowd, but I don't care. I have to do what I have to do to protect myself. I was stupid attempting this a second time. I was stupid to come all this way when even Bishop isn't here. I was stupid for giving my heart hope, both with my music career and also with the man I once lost and who won't speak to me now.

I don't care anymore.

I am a failure.

I march straight towards the door, open it, and step outside.

And run straight into the man I can't get out of my head.

"Bishop..."

He ignores me and my shock and continues past me into the boardroom, leaving me behind staring in disbelief.

I continue to watch in horror as he stands in front of all the executives and clears his voice, seizing their attention.

"Hello, everyone," he announces to the room. "I want to say something..."

## 34

*BISHOP*

CHLOE STARES at me from the doorway to the boardroom like she wants to murder me. Like, *stab me with a knife over and over and push my rotting corpse over a bridge* kind of stare.

But I ignore her and continue to talk to the room full of the most important people in American music.

"All of you *might* know who I am," I start with my hand over my heart. My line raises a few chuckles from the suits. I see Mickey Miller in the front row.

He's not laughing.

*Oh, this ain't going to be easy.*

I'm going to have to use all my charm to hold these guys' attention for a few minutes more. And I know this is the most important moment in my career so far and it's potentially career-killing, but I am willing to sacrifice my reputation to give my girl another chance to prove herself.

Because I know she can. Because I know she has the

talent in spades to blow the socks off all these stiff executives in this room.

All she has to do is perform for them and they will see her genius, I know it. She can't run away, not now. She can't afford to.

*I'm not going to let her*.

It was my fault that she's been so traumatized by live performance – that because of me she can't do this today - and it's my job now to fix it.

"But I doubt any of you know this girl here," I continue to the executives, pointing at Chloe trying to slink silently out of the room. Yep, she's still staring at me with murder in her eyes. "Or, at least, not until a few days ago when she went viral on the internet for her talent. You might not know her, but I do. We have a history, her and I, and if there's anything I know on this planet, it's music. And Chloe Stoll has that pure natural talent you all are looking for. I've spent the last few days with this musician and let me tell you that she's got notebooks full of original heartbreaking songs. Enough to fill a decade's worth of bestselling albums with. With your backing, she could be the next big voice in solo female music. The next Taylor Swift."

I take a pause to scope the vibe of the room. Judging from the quiet and the rapt looks on their faces, I've still got their attention.

For now.

"You might also know me for the little band I'm part of. Chloe was meant to be in said band as an original member until I sabotaged her chances for a petty reason. A *real* petty reason that wasn't worth the fucking time or effort. But she's spent the last seven years honing her craft behind closed doors like a true genius. The girl practically picked up a guitar as a child and was already a prodigy. You might think that she's choked up in front of you today, but I've seen her perform before. If you want any evidence of her skill, I can show you right now."

I point behind me at the boardroom's screen mounted on the wall that's usually used for boring-ass stock presentations or some shit, but today I've utilized it for a different purpose.

And these stiff suits are about to find out.

I press a button on my phone that sends a text message to Lucas – who is on the other side of the city - and immediately he flies into action. He's been waiting for my signal.

The screen lights up under my manager's remote command. The virtuoso himself takes control.

And the screen starts to play a video taken from my phone the other night.

I sneak a glance back at Chloe as she stares at herself singing Landslide at the karaoke bar, unknowing that I was filming her.

There's silence as everyone watches my recording.

*They must see and hear how damn good she is. It's undeniable.*

Chloe must see it for herself as well. She stands by the door and watches along in stunned immobility.

I wait until past Chloe has finished singing that verse when I stop the video and I turn back to the boardroom.

"Have you seen a better cover of Landslide?" I ask the room. "Have you seen such talent? So how about you give her one last chance to prove herself? How does that sound?" I then turn to Chloe still standing in the doorway. These next words, even though I'm saying them in public, are for her ears only. "I am sorry, Chloe. For everything. For sabotaging your dreams. For being the biggest idiot in the world. If I could, I'd go back in time and tell my teenage self that I'm going to lose the love of my life for one stupid act of retaliation, and that it's not worth it. I wish I could take it all back. I may be in the biggest band on the planet, but I've lost. I lost you once, and I am never going to lose you again. I am definitely *not* cooler than you."

Chloe opens her mouth to speak, but I interrupt her.

"Get your ass back up here and sing, Chloe. Show these guys what you can do."

She closes her mouth, finally understanding everything. What I'm doing.

I pray to God that she does what I ask her to do, otherwise I'm going to look like the biggest idiot in the fucking world.

But then she steps forward. Back in front of the room. She lowers her guitar into her hands as I brush past her, giving her space to perform. We don't say a word to each other.

We don't need to.

And she starts to continue singing Landslide.

I watch her from the doorway. I can't do anything else but smile goofily at her the entire time she sings that song in the most heartfelt way.

I take a glance around the boardroom. She is most *definitely* blowing the socks off these stiff suits.

She is amazing, just as I've always known she is since I first snuck into her bedroom all those years ago.

She's talented.

Beautiful.

She glances at me, mid-song, and smiles.

And I mouth back. *I don't lose.*

She blushes at that.

She's my girl.

## 35

## CHLOE

IMMEDIATELY AFTER MY performance in front of the boardroom of executives, I am offered a record deal with Mickey Miller on the spot.

It's beyond my wildest dreams.

Mickey Miller literally walks up to me, shakes my hand, and proposes it right then and there.

"I'll have my assistant call you in the next few days to arrange a meeting to formalize everything," he tells me, his fake-tanned hand strongly gripping mine. "It'll be good to work with you, Chloe Stoll. I see a very... rewarding future in store. For the both of us."

*And that's why he gets paid the big bucks.*

"Get the assistant to call my lawyers," Bishop tells the producer, butting in with that confident charm of his. "They'll look through it all, if that's okay with you, Chloe?"

I just nod. I'm still in shock from what Mickey Miller is offering me. "Sure."

The powerful producer smiles. "You were good today,

Chloe," he says. "Keep that up. I'm expecting great things from you, young lady."

When he leaves, the rest of the executive team follows him out. Bishop and I are alone in the boardroom.

I wait until they're definitely out of earshot before squealing.

"Wow," Bishop exclaims to me. "Mickey Miller said that you're *good*. That's incredible, coming from him."

"It is?"

"He never says anything like that."

"Okay. Holy shit, is this real?"

"It is," Bishop says. "Eat it up. Welcome to the big leagues."

"Everything I've ever worked for," I whisper. "All those long hours practicing on my own... not thinking anyone would hear a single note from me..."

"You really do deserve all this," Bishop says.

I look around the boardroom, and then at my guitar resting against the wall. If I really do take up this offer, then my dreams will come true. All those years of imagining.

And yet... it doesn't seem real. I'm not as ecstatic as I thought I'd be.

All I care about is Bishop. How that man just waltzed in here and simply talked the room into giving me a second chance. He risked his reputation for me.

Sure, I was angry at him at first for barging in like that all suddenly, but then I listened to what he had to say.

He *apologized* to me.

For everything he did. For the past.

And he's saved my future.

"So, you're going to take him up on his offer?" Bishop asks me. "You'd be crazy not to. It'll change your entire life."

I take a seat on one of the boardroom chairs. I need this all to sink in.

"I'll have to have a think about it," I say. "There's a lot to ponder."

"You've just been offered one of the most amazing record deals by the biggest producer in the world and you're going to *think* about it?" Bishop is incredulous. He stares at me all googly-eyed.

"There's a lot to take in. Like you said, it will change my life. Am I ready for that?"

"You're crazy, Chloe."

"Maybe I am."

"Remember, you've always got me," he says. "I can help you through this. We can do this together. I'll be there every step of the way."

"Thanks."

"Well, you've got a few days to do your thinking," he says.

I smile. "Yeah?"

"I can help you go over things if you'll like," Bishop tells me.

"Well, how about you come to mine and we can talk things over?"

* * *

WE'RE in Bishop's car, driving back to my place from Mickey Miller's office, when I finally acknowledge what the rockstar just did for me in there.

"Thanks for that," I whisper, keeping my eyes on the road. "Thank you for apologizing. Thank you for getting me back in front of those guys to perform."

Bishop puts his hand gently on my knee. "It was all you," he replies. "I just gave you the push you needed. The rest was *you*, just as I thought it would be."

And, sitting there in his car, I believe him.

He apologized to me. That's it. All over.

Like Axel tried to tell me, the past is the past. I'm finally ready to forgive and forget.

What Bishop has shown me today is that he's still in love with me. That I am his world.

He's shown me he's changed.

He's my man.

# 36

*CHLOE*

WE START KISSING before we even get through the door. I know that Gary is out today, so there's no chance of him walking in on us. And what a sight it would be for him if he does. Bishop has got me in a full embrace. He's having to lean down to kiss me, his hands running through my hair as he brings my head towards his lips. I feel so small in his arms and I'm loving it.

He lifts me up from the ground and takes me inside with just his sheer manly strength.

"You've got muscles," I say.

"I work out all day just to carry you," he replies.

We fall onto the couch in the living room, giggling like naughty schoolkids. He lies on top of me, pinning down my wrists. I stare up into his deep eyes.

He's going to say something, I just know.

"I am sorry," he whispers.

I shake my head and laugh. "I don't care anymore. Sometimes you have to move on, it's just taken me some time to properly realize that. We've wasted enough time already."

"All the pleasure is worth the pain," Bishop replies with that cheeky grin of his. "And I want my pleasure."

"You do?"

"I want to taste you."

"Tell me more."

"I want to have what's been denied to me for years, Chloe Stoll."

"And all I want from you, Bishop Hayes, is for you to fuck me right now."

"Yes, ma'am."

He delicately traces the tip of his index finger up along my jaw, stopping at my mouth. He dances over my lips. He's inviting me to suck on it, and I do. Slowly at first, and then with more vigor. The intense and barbarian way in which his deep eyes watch me suck his finger makes a heat wave shoot down my body. I feel myself slipping. Losing myself to his possession...

Seeing my eyes glaze over with desire, Bishop growls like a wolf and reaches down to kiss me ferociously. It's like he's priming to devour me. Like me finally succumbing to his physical touch is enough to drive him wild with unrestrained lust.

Well, I have no qualms with that.

My hands are still bound by one of his. He lets them go.

"Take everything off," he snarls, his voice deep and controlling.

I don't need him to tell me a second time. My hands pull up my blouse, revealing my bra.

"*Everything*," Bishop confirms. I can't help but moan at the rising bulge in his pants as he presses against my leg.

The man is insatiable.

"You want me naked?"

"I want *you*, princess."

"Yeah?"

"I want to see every part of you," he replies darkly. "You are back to where you belong, Chloe. With me."

With my bra unclasped, I reach for my pants. Bishop helps me; his hands guiding mine to unzip and unbutton. He's so eager for my flesh that it turns me on. In one movement, he rips down my jeans.

All I'm left wearing is my panties.

"I'm such an idiot for pushing you away for so long," I mutter.

Bishop is unfazed. "Let me make it up to you now."

His thumb presses down around the rim of my panties, making me gasp.

*I've never been this wet before in my entire damn life.*

Bishop leans down and kisses my collarbone. He swiftly travels down to my breasts. His tongue swirls around my erect left nipple before he pinches it between his teeth. My hands fly up to ruffle through his hair. It's completely involuntary. Bishop doesn't seem to mind. He relishes my lust for him, raising his head to grin at me.

*That grin I can't resist...*

"Let me have you," he whispers. "Finally..."

And then his mouth is traveling further down. All the way past my wetness, down to my inner thigh. He bites at my skin like he wants to eat me. My back arches and my eyes close.

His fingers trace the outline of my lips. The sensitivity is overwhelming.

*He's teasing me so bad.*

"You want me to do this?" he asks.

"Please, Bishop. Do it."

I've never begged for oral in my life, but right now I'll

get down on my knees if it meant Bishop would put himself inside me. I'm *burning* for him.

Bishop's tongue slides up my sex. He can't stop now. That'll be a crime.

My legs wrap around his head as if to trap him there. I can't help myself. Bishop continues to lightly graze the edges of my pussy, playing me like one of his goddamn instruments.

With a growl from him, one of his arms reaches out and pushes my hips down, freeing himself from between my legs. The very tip of his tongue finally makes contact with my swelling clit and I let out a cry of desperation.

*I need him inside me right now.*

Stars glow around me as the rockstar pampers my clit with the expert flickers of his tongue, driving me berserk.

The sheer severity of the pleasure I'm experiencing is too much for any one woman to handle. I find myself clawing for him. My body stiffening. My eyes rolling back.

And then it comes.

Waves of delight that wash over me. A climax like no other.

Bishop's done this. Bishop's made me feel like this.

A daze creeps over me as I cry out his name.

"Bishop..."

But the man's not done yet.

I hear a rustling of a condom packet as he rips it apart with a ferociousness of an untamed animal. His pants are down. His cock is out. He's impossibly large. He's thick. Veiny. Wide and steely.

"You've grown up since the last time I saw you naked," I whisper.

Bishop laughs at that. He pulls off his shirt, revealing his sweaty torso underneath. Those glistening, rippling muscles. There's no loss with him taking off that shirt. He was practically bursting out of it, anyway.

I catch a glimpse of us in the mirror. Bishop in all his naked glory, standing over me with his erect member like a spear threatening me. I'm all creamy white, lying down. Basking in my sluttiness.

"I've been dreaming of this for a long fucking time," Bishop snarls as he climbs on top of me.

"So have I," I breathlessly rasp. "You wouldn't believe the dreams I've had…"

"Tell me about those dreams."

"You come in," I whisper. "I protest weakly, but you take me for your own."

"Just like I'm going to do now," he snarls. "You are all mine."

"I am."

"Such a good girl."

My cheeks burn with that statement.

With one hand, he guides himself into me. I gasp as I feel a million tiny sparks light up my pussy as I accommodate his large girth. His thick, muscular body looms over me, his free hand clamoring down on my shoulder. I gaze up at his defined bicep. The *power* that courses through those veins. The musical talent that his fingers hold.

Bishop thrusts deep.

*We're connected, him and I.*

"Fuck," he exclaims. "This is better than all those dreams."

"I want you to come for me," I urge him as he rocks deeper and deeper inside me. "I want you to finish inside me."

Bishop bares his teeth at me.

"I want you to fuck me the way you've been wanting to fuck me all these years."

The man lets out a roar and his thrusts go harder.

*He's definitely been wanting to do this for so very long.*

I like the way he glares at me. That fire burning on the other side of his deep brown eyes. It makes me feel like the only girl in the world.

He makes a raw sound from the back of his throat.

"Chloe..."

And then he's finishing with an explosive climax. I shudder against him, my legs quaking as he lets go.

He falls down next to me on the bed. Both of us completely done.

I'M LYING in my bed next to my man with my finger gently circling his thick chest. He takes in deep and slow breaths. He's so hot to lie next to. Like a big hot water bottle.

I sigh.

"I'm sorry as well," I whisper.

Bishop's eyes flicker open. "About what?" he asks me.

"About telling Axel about us without getting your permission first. It was rude of me."

"Like you said," Bishop replies. "It doesn't matter anymore."

"I just wanted to tell my brother," I explain. "I wanted to tell *someone* about us. I was a girl in love. I am *still* a girl in love."

Bishop turns to me. His eyes bore into my own.

"What do you want, Chloe?"

"I just want you to cuddle me, Bishop."

He wraps his arms around me, and with just that, the years melt away and we are back to being two innocent teenagers in first love.

# 37

## BISHOP

I FLIP OVER THE PAGE, quickly scanning through the paragraphs.

"Looks alright," I say to Chloe, pointing at the contract Mickey Miller has sent through to her. It's been a few days since her performance.

My girl looks up at me with trusting eyes. She's relying on me to make sure everything's okay. "Yeah?"

"It's similar to the one I remember from the early days of Ravaged," I reply. "But I'll send it to my lawyers to have a thorough look, anyway. Have them spot any of those legal tricks and loopholes Mickey Miller might be tempted to put in for an unsigned artist."

"Okay. Thanks for that. I wouldn't know where to start with a deal this big."

"So," I start. "You think you're going to sign, then?"

Chloe bites her lip. "It's everything I've ever wanted. To be a full-time musician. No more working behind a till for me."

"That's a *yes*, right? Please say it's a yes. This is all I want for you."

She nods. "I won't deny I'm freaking terrified of everything, but I'll do it."

I bring her in for a hug. "Everything is going to change for you," I whisper. "But I'll be there. Every step of the way. Next to you. I've been through this shit myself, so I *kinda* know what it's like."

"I'll like to thank you, Bishop."

I lean back.

"You can thank me by never leaving my side again."

"Trust me," she says. "I'll *never* even think about it."

"I know what to call your debut album," I say.

Chloe's eyes light up. "What?"

"Calm Storm."

"Calm Storm?" she asks. "Why?"

"Because it's *you*," I say. "You remind me of something both raging and yet so serene."

She nods. "I like it."

I can tell she's thinking of something.

"What's on your mind?" I ask her.

Chloe bites her lip again and stares up at me with hungry eyes. Oh, how I like that look.

*I have an inkling of where this is going to go.*

"Maybe this," she says before she lowers her hands around my belt and starts to unbuckle it.

"Is your gay roommate home?" I ask her.

"No. And even if he were, I wouldn't care."

"That's hot, Chloe. Fucking hot."

"Well, I'm horny as hell, Bishop, and there's only one thing that will temper me."

"I like the sound of that," I say.

I breathe in a sigh of excitement as she brings herself to her knees in front of me as she pulls down my pants, allowing my erect cock to spring forth. She moans as she sees it. She takes my member into her mouth and begins to play with me.

Tease me.

Make me reach down and grab the top of her head as she fondles my balls.

Her sucking me off like this makes me feel like a strong man. Like she's paying me back. Like she wants me to feel damn good and powerful. She's making herself vulnerable in front of me and performing on me. And I fucking relish it.

"That's it, sexy girl," I groan as she takes my entire girth in her pretty mouth. "Bring me all in. Make me cum."

I guide her head with my hand to make her do exactly what I like. My cock feels so good between her soft lips. In no time, she brings me to the point of orgasm.

I moan her name over and over as I release inside her mouth.

"Chloe... Chloe... Chloe..."

She swallows me as I tilt my head back and bask in my climax.

*Fuck. She's damn good.*

"I remember those sweet lips," I breathlessly whisper as I buckle up my pants. Chloe rises and I kiss those same lips.

"Oh, you do?"

"You're being very cheeky," I reply. "I've gotta do something about that."

"Please do."

She smiles as I grab her arms and spin her around. I lift her into the air and onto her bed, spreading her legs and ferociously pulling down her panties so that I can see her sex.

"My turn," I snarl as I lower myself to kiss her other sweet lips between her legs. Chloe arches her back and groans loudly. The noise she makes is so fucking hot that I can't stop myself now. My tongue traces the outline of her pussy as my fingers stroke the soft skin of her inner thigh. I sense her whole body tense up and relax in pleasure as I take my time to gently torment her.

"Stop teasing me," she whispers from the top of the bed.

I ignore her and continue my tongue's slow dance towards her clit. I quickly dab it with the tip of my tongue as Chloe's hands try to pull my face in closer to her pussy. She *needs* me. And I'm going to take my sweet ass time.

This girl... Her taste...

*Fuck me.*

"Do you want me to do this?" I ask her, breathless from my effort.

"Don't you fucking dare stop, Bishop..."

I glance up at her. She sees the primal lust in my eyes. I can't wait to conquer her. Taste her pleasure yet again.

She turns me on like no other woman has. No other woman could do.

I dive back in, slowly tracing her soaking wet lips. This is heaven, and she is eternity.

She lets out an ear-shattering moan that's pure bliss. I love making her feel like this. I love the music she unwillingly produces from her mouth as I gently tease her with my own mouth. The tip of my tongue dabs in tiny circles over her inviting clit. Her hand clenches my own as she reaches the point of ecstasy.

*The power I have over her right now...*

I can practically see the stars radiating off her as I bring her to an explosive climax. Her whole body arches in uncontrollable pleasure as I plunder her treasures simply with the edges of my tongue.

"Oh God, Bishop. Oh my God."

She yanks at my hair as her breathing slows from the waves of delight that pass through her.

My cock is practically leaking now. I need to fuck her.

Chloe raises her head to look down at me, still between her legs. I bare my teeth at her. "Delicious."

"Oh, Bishop."

"And now I'm going to fuck you."

Chloe makes a groan of longing. If nothing else will turn me on, this certainly does.

"I'm guessing you want me to get inside you?"

"Please."

That's all I need to start fishing for a condom. With it quickly around my shaft, I mount Chloe and enter her in a fast movement.

"I am so hungry for you," I moan as I pump in deep and slow. Her wet sex firmly adjusts itself to my length.

"I love how much you need me," she rasps back.

"You wouldn't believe. Every piece of me is angling for you. Every piece of me *needs* you."

"Every piece of me is for you."

That sends me over the fucking cliff. My body stiffens in a primitive urge and then I come, groaning. Every piece of me is taut. I grunt through my gritted teeth as I'm blown apart inside this woman.

Chloe's bright green eyes stare at me as I climax, spurring me on to even greater heights.

I've never felt so attached to someone as in this moment. As if our two souls ascended from our physical bodies and rearrange themselves as one in the stars above.

Yeah, it's definitely true no single girl has made me feel like this before.

"Chloe Stoll," I whisper after I'm gone. "You have every fucking piece of me."

# 38

*CHLOE*

I RING the bell and I'm not waiting for long before Maddie opens the front door with her cute little bashful smile. I am here at her invitation.

"Hi!"

"I was thinking of having a girl's day," she says as she ushers me inside her and Axel's place. "Just us two."

She seems so happy I'm here, the introverted angel. I smile back at her in gratitude.

"Thanks for messaging."

"Oh, no bother. I've wanted some proper one-on-one time with you," my brother's girlfriend replies. "Especially now that you've been so busy with Bishop and your music."

She raises a curious eyebrow at that last sentence as if to inquire with just an expression. I can't help but break eye contact and blush.

"You know something's going on between us?" I ask.

*Guilty.*

I've not spoken about Bishop and me and us together

again to *anyone*, but it seems like smart Maddie has sniffed things out.

*She's too good.*

She pats me on the back. "Come on, Chloe, you should know as well as anyone the Ravaged boys aren't hard to read," she replies coyly. "Bishop has suddenly become a lot happier these last few days, and you have completely and mysteriously disappeared from all contact; I don't have to be Sherlock Holmes to connect the dots presented before me."

I laugh. "You are perceptive, Maddie, I'll give you that."

"So I got it right? Exciting."

"Please don't make a song and dance about it."

She crosses her heart. "I swear I won't tell a soul."

"Thanks."

"Please sit," she says, gesturing to her couch. She asks me what drink I'll like.

It's when she brings me a coffee that I ask her how the pregnancy is going, hoping to change the subject from Bishop and me.

"How is the baby?"

Maddie swats away my question. "Oh, all good, but I want to hear about you and Bishop. You can't hide this from me, Chloe. With Ravaged, I feel like I've entered into a never-ending soap opera and I can't get enough now. My life was so boring before Axel strutted in and ruined it."

"Yeah, those boys do lead pretty dramatic lives."

"You don't say," Maddie replies with a wink. "I live vicariously through them and they provide hours of entertainment. So, tell me about you two. Give me the gossip."

I decide to tell her everything. I mean, she is the only person on the planet who might understand what it's like to be head-over-heels in love with an international rock god, so I know I can trust her. No one else could possibly understand what it's like to be with someone from Ravaged.

I let her know everything that's passed between Bishop and me. All our backstory and everything that's happened these last few crazy days. From me hating his guts to him saving my career. The entire whirlwind.

"And so," I conclude. "I've signed the contract and now I'm going to make an album with Mickey Miller's team."

Maddie's face drops into shock. "Wow, Chloe. You're going to be a star."

I blush again. "Well, we'll see about that. I need to put in the work first..."

"For sure you are," she replies, rubbing my knees affectionately. "And what I love most is you and Bishop being back together. You seem so happy by it. I can literally see it on your face when you talk about him. You're in love, Chloe. And, my God, you should see what he's been acting like these last few days when he's come around to be with Axel. That man is ecstatic. He's acting like he's God's own gift to the world. That's all *you*."

"Well, the sex has been pretty damn crazy," I remark, and we both fall into a fit of giggles.

"You two have picked up the pieces from seven years ago," Maddie says, snorting. "That must be pretty hot to rediscover someone's body like that."

"Yeah. It's steamy."

"Now this I need to find out more..."

I snort. "I thought you were pretty shy?"

"I gotta get my fix somewhere, Chloe. As I said, Ravaged is like a live soap opera happening before my eyes."

The doorbell rings.

Our heads turn to the front of the house in unison.

"I wasn't expecting anyone," Maddie says. She gets up from the couch and heads down the hallway.

A moment later, I hear the door open and then high-pitched noises that sound like squealing. I twist my head to try to catch a glance down the hallway, but Maddie reappears before I can see what the hell's going on.

"This might be a surprise," she tells me, breathless. "But look who's here."

She points behind her at whoever's just entered.

It's Mom.

## 39

*CHLOE*

"Mom?"

She immediately rushes across Maddie's living room to wrap her long arms around me. I embrace her back, but my mouth still hangs open.

*I can't believe this...*

She looks like Mom. She smells like Mom. It *must* be Mom.

"Chloe!"

"Did you know about this?" I ask Maddie, my body still tightly constrained by my mother's hug. My brother's girlfriend shakes her head in response.

"It's good to see you, Chloe," Mom says. "And you too, Maddie."

"Always lovely to see you, Astrid."

"What are you doing here?" I ask Mom as I successfully wriggle free from her grasp.

"Axel told me you'd be here," she replies with a wink.

"He was told by Bishop. All roads lead back to me, daughter."

"You're very good at collecting information on us, aren't you? I can't hide from you, even if I try."

"You know me."

"But you hate Los Angeles."

"So do you, Chloe."

"Yeah, but I'm not the one who's visited it twice in such a short amount of time," I point out. "First you came to see Maddie for the first time, now it's to see me..."

"Both great reasons to come," Mom says, winking again. This time at Maddie. "Both my children have made me so incredibly proud, so why wouldn't I come? Especially when you're in the same freaking city for once."

I roll my eyes. "I'm guessing Axel's told you everything about the last few days, has he?"

"He got that information from Bishop."

"Ah, so there is a rat. You are really very good, Mom."

"But I want to hear everything from the horse's mouth, Chloe. You and Bishop. Everything. Now."

"Should I get popcorn?" Maddie jokes.

I blush. "What do you want to know, Mom?"

"Maybe start at the fact he broke your heart, and yet, apparently, you're back together..."

And so I recount to my mother, in detail, all the craziness of the last few days. Well, maybe not *all* the details. Mom doesn't need to know *how* much I like Bishop. But I tell her everything she needs to know.

We are so enamored with catching up that Mom and I don't even move. We're still standing by the time I tell her about the performance in front of Mickey Miller and being offered the record deal.

She immediately wraps her arms around me again.

"I knew you'd reach your dreams one day," she whispers into my ear. "I'm *so, so, so, so* proud of you, Chloe."

"Thanks, Mom."

"And what does the future hold for you and Bishop?" she asks me.

I shrug. "Hopefully... everything."

"Sounds perfect."

"Would you like something to drink?" Maddie asks my mother, guiding her to sit down on the couch.

"Oh, I don't know. What are you girls having?"

"I'm having a sparkling water," Maddie replies. "On account of the whole little pregnancy thing I've got going."

"But I'm going to have a glass of white," I reply. Might as well get stuck into the alcohol now that Mom's swanned in so dramatically.

"Wine it is, then."

As Maddie so kindly fetches us both a glass of wine, I turn to my Mom.

"Where are you staying, then?"

"I've booked myself into a hotel. Cute little place. Axel found it for me."

"Oh, right."

"I'm not planning to stay for long, but I'm happy to just see both my children in the same place for once. You never come here and Axel never comes to Crystal River."

"True."

"Why do you hate Los Angeles?" Maddie asks Mom as she returns with our glasses. "I know there's unfinished business between you and Winston West, but you still haven't told me anything about that."

"Going in straight with the deep questions," Mom replies with a cheeky smile that reminds me too much of Axel. "I like that, Maddie."

"Who's Winston West?" I blurt out, completely

confused by this line of conversation.

But I'm not sure I'm going to like where this is all leading to.

"He's my former boss at the publicity company I worked at," Maddie explains. "He was the guy that paired me up with Axel and Ravaged. Last I heard, Astrid and him have got some history together, although she has been very keen on keeping those secrets quite close to her chest. I've yet to wrangle any of the gossip from her."

Mom tries to wave it all away. "It was a long time ago, long before I met your father."

I spin around to my mother. "History? With a man? Before Dad? You've got to tell me all about this. Right now."

My mother takes a long sigh and then speaks. "Fine, then. I will."

"We're all ears," Maddie says. I agree wholeheartedly. We both lean in to express how eager we are to hear this tale.

"Okay," Mom starts. "To set the scene... I once lived, in a time long before Chloe and Axel, in this city as a groupie bouncing around the music scene. Remember, I was young and free and wild at heart back then, very different from the wise, mature woman I am now. I loved that period of my life. I had my routine down perfectly. I would attach myself to some famous band and just let myself be dragged along for the ride. The eighties were a very fun time for me, I have to say. And so we get onto Winston West..."

"The good part," Maddie exclaims, her eyes sparkling at the thought. I have to admit it's kind of hilarious hearing my mother talk about her past like this. As a kid, she never spoke of her time before Dad. Maybe now I'm older – much older – she's decided that I'm finally of the age to be allowed to be privy to her *young, free, and wild* days.

I'm not complaining, though. This is all

so *very* interesting.

"Winston West was a roadie for bands back then, long before he moved into marketing," Mom continues. "He did everything for a band. Helped them carry their stuff. Worked on the lights. Even did security some nights. We moved in the same crowds and let's just say, long story short, that something led to another and something blossomed between us for a few months. It got to the point where I started to delude myself and thought it had the potential to be something serious. The be-all and end-all. But then he went on tour. He asked me to wait for him when he returned. I waited for six months but *nada*. Nothing. He didn't come back. Remember, these were the days before the internet. It was just like he vanished into thin air. *Poof*."

"And he never came back?" Maddie asks.

"Nope."

"Crazy," I remark. "I really didn't know any of this about you, Mom."

"So, heart broken, I moved back to my hometown of Crystal River. I met your dad, Chloe. I had my kids and family. And then your dad passed away."

"You never saw Winston again until you were last here?" Maddie asks.

"Never. Not until that restaurant here where we happened to bump into each other. That was one big hell of a shock, let me tell you."

"Wow," I say. "Some story. Did he apologize for disappearing on you?"

Mom sighs again. "No."

"And if he did apologize, would you take him back?" I ask.

My mother pauses for a long time before she answers.

"He'll never apologize. Men like him don't like to realize their mistakes."

# 40

## BISHOP

A LITTLE BIT DRUNK, and definitely a little bit horny, Chloe persistently knocks on my door. Loudly. She doesn't stop until I answer it.

She scoffs dismissively and mockingly at my serious expression when I finally open up.

"Oh, hello, mister Hayes. Fancy meeting you around these parts."

"Yeah, my house is a strange place to find me."

"Such a joker," she giggles. "I always liked that about you."

"I know you've been out all day at Maddie's," I tell her. "Had a good time?"

"Oh, for sure, yes."

"I can tell."

Yeah, she's *definitely* a little bit drunk. Maybe a decent amount. She's swaying on her feet and giggling playfully to herself. She seems to be having lots of fun.

I let her inside. She's unsteady as she enters, looking around.

"Your place certainly needs a woman's touch, Bishop."

"And you think you're the woman to make that happen?"

She dramatically places a hand over her heart and launches into a very poor rendition of a posh English accent. "Me? Why, thank you, kind sir. I will *gladly* take you up on your offer, you gentleman."

"Just get inside, woman."

I take her by the waist and guide her into the kitchen. Chloe loves that I'm touching her like this. She bites her lips and stares at my muscular arm.

"Why, what big arms you have. You're showing me the way?"

"I'll throw you over my shoulder in a minute if you don't behave," I growl.

She really likes that.

"I'll be on my worst behavior," she says, poking me in the ribs to get my attention.

I'm going to tease her for a bit. I'm not going to do what she wants just because she's horny.

I mean, so am I. But I'm always hard around this girl.

"Sit down," I say, nodding at one of my kitchen stools.

"Yes, sir."

I head to the fridge and get myself a beer. I better catch up to Chloe's drunken level.

"Oh, getting yourself a beer," Chloe coos. She thinks she's being testing. I'll show her testing in a minute.

"Was it just you and Maddie, then?" I ask her. "You two having a girls' day?"

"Guess what? My mom turned up."

I nearly spit out my beer. "Astrid? She's in LA?"

"What other mom would I be talking about, silly? Yes,

Astrid. Axel and mine mother. The woman who gave birth to me."

*The alcohol is making her bold, I see.*

"Yeah?"

"She told us about some guy she used to see way before Axel and I came along. It's kind of a cute story, actually. You know, I reckon it would be really nice for my mom to meet this guy again."

"I don't really understand what you're saying, Chloe. How about I get you some nice cold water?"

"That would be wonderful."

I roll my eyes and get her a glass. She starts talking non-stop now. Drunkenly running her mouth.

"It's so good I signed that contract," she says. "I'm so excited for what's to come. I want to thank you again, Bishop, for helping me with it all."

"I put you in the right direction, that's all. You're the one who has the talent."

"Damn right," she replies.

"And what are you planning to do now, Chloe? What's your living situation going to be like?"

Maybe I'll get an honest answer from her. I don't want her to leave. The last few days have been the best of my life. I can't let her go a second time.

"I'm going to stay with Gary," she says.

"The gay guy?"

"Yeah, the *gay* guy. He's offered to rent me that room for a while until everything is sorted out with Mickey Miller and stuff. I've had a phone call with his team and we're already coming up with ideas for the album and everything."

I nod. "That's a good thing to do."

"Damn right it is."

"But I'm going to make you a counter-offer," I say.

"What?"

"You're free to stay with me instead of with Gary."

"Oh, am I?"

"If you want."

"But aren't you going to be a distraction for me?"

"I'm going to be a *big* distraction."

Chloe gets up from the stool and strides towards me, strutting her hips seductively.

"How big?" she asks.

"Very," I reply.

"How about putting that big pool of yours to a use other than swimming?" she asks me quietly, using her finger to hook around the collar of my shirt and bringing my face towards her mouth.

Before I kiss her, I reach for my bottle on the counter. "In that case, I'll need another beer."

## 41

*BISHOP*

SHE'S A BIT DRUNK, but that doesn't stop her from stripping down completely naked, leading me to my pool out the back of my place, and being the first one to dive straight in. Hair wet and everything.

It's pretty damn sexy.

"Take those briefs off," Chloe calls at me from the pool, her voice echoing around my vast backyard. Her wet lips look so sweet and so damn inviting from up here. I'm standing by the edge in nothing but my Calvin Klein's, and it's pretty damn obvious - even without her words - she wants them gone. Right now.

"I don't dare disobey an order."

I reach down and, just like that, those briefs are off, just as Chloe wishes. And like my girl bobbling up and down in the pool, I am completely naked. Chloe admires my erect cock with lustful eyes. That turns me on even more.

But I don't go into the water just yet.

Instead, I lean over for a remote strategically placed by

the edge of the pool. I point it down at my feet and press the button right in the middle of the remote.

And just like that, my pool lights up. All around the edges are a series of underwater lights that bathe the thing in a luminous glow. Chloe's lustful eyes shine as she takes an approving look around.

And then the music starts. A deep bass from outdoor speakers located all around.

I had this setup done when I moved into the place. It cost me the same as a small house in this neighborhood to have it installed, but *damn*, is every penny spent worth the wowed expression on Chloe's face.

"Oh, that's very cool," she says. "I like this place. Maybe I will stay. It ain't half bad."

I smile and slip into the water, coming up to her gracefully.

The water is warm, not cold. I'm tall enough that I can stand up whilst Chloe must swim to stay afloat. I take her in my arms.

And I claim my kiss.

"You know how to seduce a woman, don't you?" Chloe asks as our lips part.

I smile and draw her closer with my hand. Under the water, her body starts to dance to the music I have playing. She wills me on with a flicker of her eyes. I can't help but move with her. We're floating in the illuminated pool, our legs wrapped around each other, dancing to music.

"You know how to make a man dance," I repeat back at her before leaning in for another wet kiss. Chloe eagerly kisses back. She tastes of alcohol and water and desire. Her hips rub against mine, sending a message that's completely decipherable.

Her hand finds my erect cock. She works me hard, making me close my eyes with pleasure. My mouth clenches as she gently kisses my jaw and her right hand squeezes me below the surface of the water.

"I want you to give it to me," she whispers as she plays me like an instrument. "I want you to give it to me right here in this pool, right now."

My nostrils flare as I take in a long blast of air.

My desire for her is unhinged. My awareness of her is on fire. I am so fucking turned on.

"Fuck," I snarl before I use my hands to pull her up in the water so that her legs wrap around my hips. "I'm going to take you here, Chloe."

She leans her head back and cries out as my cock enters her. She's so willing for me. So supple to my touch. So fucking inviting. She rides my thrusts, smothering my body with her sex. Heat pulsates through me.

"I'm burning for you," I groan through gritted teeth.

"Fuck me harder," she says back, her eyes closing as she succumbs to my hold.

And so I do fuck her harder. All the way to oblivion. All the way to orgasm.

It feels like the water will take us as we ride each other. My thrusts penetrating deep inside her. The waves of the pool are like the waves of pleasure that row through me.

"*Bishop*," Chloe calls out as I let go.

Her cry of my name feeds the urge within me, and my whole body stiffens under the water as I finish.

We end up floating with the water. No longer in control. Simply kissing each other with wet lips as the music plays and the lights dim.

# 42

*CHLOE*

Mom is insistent that she takes Axel and me out for lunch the day after I stumble back to Bishop's place and have wild crazy sex in his pool. She messages me in the morning and I, extremely hungover and bleary-eyed in Bishop's bed, agree to the lunch date.

Axel picks the spot. An upmarket sushi bar in Venice Beach. Very cool and trendy and *very* LA.

Bishop kindly drops me off in his car. He gives me a long kiss before I dare get out of the vehicle. This morning he made me coffee and breakfast in bed. Bacon and scrambled eggs on sourdough. It was delicious. He treats me so well.

"Did you have fun last night, honey?" he asks me as I open the door.

I turn to meet his gaze. My body shivers at the use of the word *honey*. It shouldn't have the effect it has on me, but I can't help it. Everything tingles at the sound of his low baritone.

"Yeah, just a little," I reply, teasing.

"Maybe I'll make you have a little more fun tonight," Bishop replies. "I want you to think of me *all* day."

"I can't help it," I whisper as I lean over and kiss him again, wanting to leave him something to think about all day.

I want to stay right here in his car. I don't ever want to leave his sight.

Axel's wearing a baseball cap over his eyes in an effort to remain anonymous, but it doesn't work on me. I spot him standing outside the sushi place straight away.

"Wow, Axel Stoll, right here!" I make a big noise as I rush up and hug him. He glares at me, seething.

"Chloe, I'm trying not to get recognized. Otherwise, this place will be swarming with people wanting selfies in a matter of seconds."

"Lighten up, Mr. Ego," I scoff, nudging him.

"Stop fighting, you two." Mom stealthily appears by our side. Both Axel and I give her a big hug.

"Hello, mother," Axel grumbles. The man might try to appear dead cool, but underneath all that bravado and male charisma, he's still a little boy who loves his mom.

Mom takes our hands and sighs happily. "I am so happy to see both of you," she says with a beam across her face. "I am so proud of what you've both accomplished in your own way."

Underneath the baseball cap, I see a flicker of blush on Axel's perfect cheeks. "Let's go inside," he hastily suggests.

"Can't handle a bit of love from your mom?" I ask him. It's so fun to give him a little ribbing.

"Let's. Go. Inside."

We sit down by the window booth, watching the unique sights of Venice Beach pass us by as we eat enough sushi to feed a small army. I have to hand it to him; Axel's picked a great spot here. You wouldn't be able to get sushi like this back in Crystal River.

"It seems like you all had a merry time yesterday," Axel remarks to us. "According to Maddie."

"Oh no," I say. "What did she tell you?"

"Don't panic, her lips are sealed. Well, except for one name. *Winston West*. Does that ring a bell, Mom? I'm sure it must."

My mother's face drops.

"You know exactly who he is, Axel. He's done publicity for your band."

"There's more to him than simply a job title, isn't there?"

Mom laughs then. "I am here to see you both, not to meet up with some guy from decades ago."

"So you're keeping your lips sealed as well, Mom?"

"I certainly am, Axel."

\* \* \*

AXEL OFFERS to drive us both home to our respective places. Mom to her hotel. Me to Bishop's.

It's when we drop Mom outside her accommodation when Axel turns to me in the passenger seat.

"You know Maddie is cooking up some plan to get Mom and Winston in the same room?" he asks me.

My jaw opens. "No, I did not know that. Sneaky girl."

"She's unwilling to pull the trigger unless you're involved, though, and you give your approval."

"I bet."

"What do you think?"

I cross my arms. "No, what do *you* think, Axel? I'm sure you have an opinion on all of this. You're her son."

"Well, what I've heard is that Mom used to be a wild

girl in her younger years. It might be good for her to experi-ence some of that youth again..."

I smile. "She *has* been on her own since Dad."

"Exactly."

I scratch my chin, pondering over it for a moment. "I mean, we can try. Mom is pretty strong-headed, though. If she truly doesn't want to see him again, then she'll just walk out of any situation Maddie and us puts her in. We won't be able to stop her from leaving."

"I hope she doesn't get angry at us."

I chortle. "Scared of Mom, are you? Such a big boy."

"Aren't you?"

"Yeah, I am a bit scared of her," I admit.

"Exactly."

I chuckle. "You know Mom, Axel. She wouldn't be. She'll find it hilarious, whatever we do."

"But one thing's for sure," my brother adds. "I don't want my publicist as my new stepdad."

That really makes my smile widen as I think of all the possibilities. "You've really convinced me there, Axel. I'm on Maddie's side now. Anything to annoy you. Let's go and see her and figure out what she's cooking up."

# 43

*CHLOE*

BISHOP IS PLAYING his guitar when I get home. I can hear the notes echoing out even before I get through the door.

"Good lunch?" he asks as I walk in, stopping his music.

I nod and begin to strip. "I'm so sweaty. It's hot outside. I think I'll have a shower."

The rockstar admires my near-naked body, but he begins to play again instead of doing anything about his obvious desire.

And so I head straight past him to the shower. I'm serious. I am sweaty. I need a wash.

Bishop, true to form, has a state-of-the-art bathroom. Well, technically he's got three. This one is massive. The shower cubicle is bigger than my own bathroom back home. I run the water and step inside.

I let myself breathe and relax. The room quickly fills with steam as the hot water washes down my back. I can't see out of the cubicle through all the mist.

But I do hear the bathroom door open. And then close.

And suddenly Bishop is in the shower. He touches me from behind, his hands running up and down my arms. His hard erection pressing against my buttocks makes it very clear the man is naked.

*That was faster than I thought it would be...*

My body shudders at Bishop's touch. His hot breath mixes with the steam and the water on the back of my neck and he leans in from behind to whisper deep in my ear.

"You think you can just swan into my house, get naked, and go in my shower without me noticing, you bad girl?"

"Hm. Maybe not."

His hand drifts slowly southward until he's cupping my ass. His grip is strong and full of lust.

"You're such a tease, Chloe."

*Damn.*

"Then do something about it, rockstar."

"Oh, I am planning to."

He pushes me against the wall of the shower.

He takes control.

Immediately, two fingers work their way into my soft, wet sex. My head rolls back onto his firm, muscular shoulder. His fingers perform some kind of magic inside me, urging me to rock into him. His engorged cock grazes my side and I gulp as I imagine the depth of his lust for me at this moment. He's a mountain of a man behind me.

I moan as his fingers tighten their hold inside me.

"You can do all of this with just your two fingers," I say in both a question of amazement and a comment of wonderment, my voice unsteady due to what he's eliciting from deep inside me.

"I can do a hell of a lot more," he replies, voice deep.

*How can I resist that gorgeous baritone?*

"Show me," I whisper in anticipation.

I feel that thick cock of his against my thigh, and I begin to understand how exactly he's about to show me...

\* \* \*

MADDIE CALLS me as Bishop has his arms wrapped tightly around me in bed. He's asleep as my phone vibrates. I struggle against his cuddle to reach for my phone on the bedside table.

Maddie is practically breathless with hurried excitement when I answer.

"I've got a brilliant plan, Chloe."

"Axel did tell me you're cooking up something to do with Mom and your former boss..."

"Yes, I am."

"Okay, I'm taking the bait. What is it?"

Maddie enthusiastically speeds through the plan.

"Alright, the deal is to hold a little party at Axel's and my place to celebrate the pregnancy. I'm going to invite both Astrid and Winston without them knowing the other is coming. *Boom*. Done. Get them together. It'll be like a scene out of a romance movie. Imagine it."

"I'm imagining it. Sounds like it'll either go like a movie or like some viral video where Mom rejects the poor man in front of everyone and storms off..."

"It will work, trust me. Of course, for this party, I will want you to be there. To sing."

My snort is loud enough to wake up Bishop. "Sing?"

"Well, you are a singer, aren't you? You did just sign a contract with the biggest producer in music, haven't you? I will love to hear you live, and I'm sure it'll help the atmosphere for your mother to meet Winston again. Think about yourself being the composer for this romantic movie."

"Wow, Maddie, you've got this all planned out, haven't you? You're one smart cookie."

I can practically hear her smile through the phone. "Oh, yes I have. So what do you say? You in?"

44

*BISHOP*

I can see that Chloe is internally freaking the fuck out even before we pull up to the front door of Maddie and Axel's.

"I'm here, Chloe."

She looks up at me with her soft, pretty eyes and I feel a pang of care in my heart. "I know. Thanks, Bishop."

"You gonna be okay?" I ask her.

She appears to be on the verge of hyperventilating, but she puts on a brave, stoic face for me. "Yeah. All good."

"Because I'll be right beside you. All the way."

She nods, and I take that as my cue that she doesn't want us to talk about her current state of nerves anymore. We head up to the front door.

Both Maddie and Axel answer.

"It's crazy seeing you both together," Chloe's brother says as he spies the two of us. A flash of guilt hits me when I think of how strong his reaction was when Chloe first told him about us all those years ago. Axel has certainly come a long way since then.

"It wasn't very long ago when Chloe wanted to kill you," Maddie adds. "Slowly."

"We've resolved a lot these last few days," I reply to the couple as I wink at Chloe. "A lot."

She glares at my innuendo.

They invite us inside. The house is all set up for the party. Balloons and canapes are all prepared. There's a mini stage set up in the living room.

"That's where you're going to sing," Maddie tells Chloe, nudging her on the elbow.

Chloe stares at it. She can't hide her nerves.

"You'll be fine," I whisper in her ear when Maddie and Axel move on. I reach down and squeeze her hand with mine for reassurance.

Soon the other members of Ravaged arrive. Drake and Caspian come together, both bounding through the door and lighting up the room in their different ways.

"Hello, all," Drake greets with his cheeky grin. He takes a look at Chloe and me. He wants to laugh at finding us together like this, and I dare him to with my glare. He gets the message and keeps his little annoying mouth shut.

Caspian heads over to Chloe and shakes her hand in his gruff, formal way. "Nice to see you again, Chloe."

"Nice to see you too, Caspian."

He then wraps his arms around her in the biggest bear hug I've ever seen. Chloe laughs as the giant man squeezes the life out of her.

"This is why you're my favorite, Caspian."

Maddie and Axel offer us all drinks. The party is still a while away from starting properly, but it was good for them to invite us early.

It's good to spend time with everyone. I watch my girl as

we call cheers with our drinks and catch up. Chloe seems happy, and that makes me happy.

The conversation quickly turns to Astrid. Chloe has filled me in on Maddie's plans.

"Do you think she'll be okay with all this?" Maddie asks as she glances around at the decorations, now feeling the nerves.

"She doesn't know it's for her," I say. "And that makes it hilarious."

Chloe elbows me. "It isn't hilarious, Bishop."

"I fully agree with Bishop," Drake adds. "I can't believe we're doing this. What do you think, Caspian?"

"I'm just here for free drinks."

"And what about you, Axel?" Drake asks. "Surely you have some opinions on this crazy plan..."

My bandmate shrugs. "We'll see what happens," he replies diplomatically.

"I have no real expectations anyway," Maddie says. "It's *just* a party and they will both be here. That's all. We can do nothing more than that. If they don't want to speak to each other, then that's perfectly fine."

"What do you reckon she'll do?" I ask Axel and Chloe.

"Mom is an independent woman who makes her own choices," my girl replies. "We can't force her or anything. She'll walk straight out if she doesn't want him."

"And then we'll be in trouble," Axel adds.

"Yep, we'll most certainly be in trouble," Chloe says.

"What song are you going to sing?" Maddie asks Chloe.

My girl looks up at me, hesitant. "I've got a little song I've written for Bishop. It's brand new, even Bishop hasn't heard it yet."

Well. This is news to me.

## 45

*CHLOE*

I HAVE BEEN SO DAMN reluctant about this party. The last thing I want is to ambush my poor mother, but when everything is in full swing and the party is underway, my worries start to dissolve.

It's a good party. Mom isn't going to feel ambushed.

I hope.

Maddie has invited a few people here. Around twenty or so friends she's made in Los Angeles since dating Axel. There's even a short bubbly girl from her old work called Marie, who first introduced Maddie to Ravaged before she even met Axel. All Marie wants to do is swoon over the Ravaged boys; following them around like a lovesick puppy. Hey, I don't blame her.

When Mom finally arrives, she heads over to Bishop and me with a warm smile.

"You two are looking very cute," she says, her eyes flickering over the rockstar and me.

I blush. "Stop it, Mom."

"Always knew you two were good together."

"Thank you, Miss Stoll." Gee, Bishop knows how to sweet-talk my mother. She likes him, I can tell.

"Okay, knock it off," I say to Mom. "Have a drink. Go and enjoy yourself."

She heads off to speak with Caspian, and I grimace at Bishop.

"It's good, right?" I ask him. "We're not bad people to ambush her?"

"It's a good party," Bishop replies, practically reading my mind. "Everyone is having a good time. She'll be fine."

"We'll see when Winston gets here. If he does."

"Well, hello, Chloe."

I recognize that loud voice anywhere.

I spin around. "Gary! You made it."

And there he is, my former roommate. He bounces over with his jolly face.

"I wouldn't miss seeing you for the world," he says in his booming voice.

His boisterous energy can't help but make me grin from ear to ear. "Have a drink," I say. "Make yourself at home."

"Oh, I am certainly planning to."

My former roommate glances at Bishop. They both stare each other down.

*Oh, right.* I forgot the weird animosity they have with each other. How Bishop is so possessive of me that he was actually *suspicious* of a gay man as my roommate.

"Gary." Bishop nods.

"Mr. Hayes," Gary replies in an equally serious tone.

"I don't think I thanked you for looking after Chloe when she moved here," my boyfriend says, offering out his hand. "So, thank you."

*Holy shit.*

Gary smiles and shakes the rockstar's hand. "It was no problem. I love the girl and I want what's best for her."

"You and me both."

"Can I just say," Gary begins. "That I am a huge fan of your music."

Bishop smiles. "I like you. How about I get you a drink, Gary? I'll introduce you to my band's manager. I think you two will get along famously..."

I watch in utter amazement as the two men stroll off, practically arm-in-arm. Gary flicks his head around and flashes a wink at me.

I can't believe those two. All that weird tension and now they get along like a house on fire.

It gives me a moment free to scan the room checking for any signs of Maddie's boss. None so far.

In my worries, I very nearly forget that I've been commissioned to sing until Maddie appears by my side.

"Have you seen him yet?" I ask her.

"Nothing."

"Well, Mom's here."

"We can't keep stalling forever," she tells me, nodding towards the makeshift stage. "It's time. I'll introduce you."

"Okay."

*Oh, here goes.*

Maddie gets up to the microphone and gets everyone's attention.

"I am so happy you all were able to make it this evening," she says. "Thank you for coming."

I glance around the room. Someone new enters. A middle-aged man.

Bishop nudges me. "That's Winston," he whispers in my ear.

I nod.

*Finally.*

I guessed as much.

"My new friend and sort-of-sister, Chloe Stoll, is going to perform for you now," Maddie announces, gesturing towards me. "She's going to be the next big star in music, so count yourselves lucky you've seen her today."

I blush again. Bishop squeezes my hand. Thank God he's here beside me. I honestly don't know what I would do without his calm, confident support.

I jump onto the stage and take over the microphone from Maddie.

"Break a leg," she tells me as she passes.

Before I start to sing, I take in a long, deep breath and glance around the crowd.

I see Mom. I see Winston. I see the members of Ravaged.

*This is your passion. This is what you've been put on this planet to do. This is what you love.*

And then I sing.

*I was lost*
*I've been found*
*A million things*
*I thought would happen*
*But this is the best of all*

*You were there*
*From the start, from the beginning*
*Why did we never think*
*Why did we pretend*
*it wasn't important*

*Because this is where*
*we're supposed to be*
*A million things*
*I thought would happen*
*But this is the best of all*

MADDIE RUSHES up to me after the performance when I join Bishop for a glass of wine.

"You did so good," she tells me enthusiastically. "Thank you."

I look at Bishop. "I wouldn't argue with that comment," he says.

I let out a sigh of relief. I *did* do good. I really came into my own on there. Everyone applauded me. The world didn't end. No one laughed me off stage.

Maybe things do change. Maybe I am no longer traumatized performing live.

*And I have Bishop to thank for that.*

My man is looking at something over both of our heads. "You wouldn't believe what's happening," he says.

"What?" both Maddie and I ask him, turning in the direction of his gaze.

"Astrid and Winston are talking."

I spot them across the room. Mom. Talking to that Winston guy.

*Wow.*

And she doesn't look like she's going to slap his face. He says something to her, and she actually *freaking* laughs. She then reaches out and touches his shoulder.

"Is she... *flirting*?" Maddie asks.

"Yes," I reply. "I think she is."

*So I guess she isn't going to kill us after all.*

Maybe this has all turned out alright.

There's sudden feedback on the microphone. I cusp my ears and turn back towards the stage.

Axel is up there.

"Hi, everyone," he says. "Can I have your attention, please?"

*What the hell's happening now?*

# 46

*CHLOE*

"Maddie, can you come up here?" Axel says into the microphone, silencing the entire party. Everyone turns to him, except for his girlfriend.

She's looking at me.

"What's he doing?" she asks me, whispering.

I shake my head. I don't have a clue what my brother is trying to do.

*Embarrass her? I think so, knowing him.*

But Axel is gesturing for her to join him on the stage, not giving up. And Maddie reluctantly agrees to join him.

My brother smiles when his pregnant girlfriend comes up in front of everyone. He runs his hands through his wavy black hair.

"Can I just say, Maddie, that you look so incredibly beautiful right now," he says in his low voice.

Everyone's enraptured by what's occurring.

Maddie shakes her head at him nervously, but that

doesn't deter Axel in the slightest. She's a withdrawn girl, not used to being the center of attention, unlike her flamboyant rockstar boyfriend.

"I want to stop the party for just one moment, if you all will let me," he continues into the microphone as if he hasn't stopped the entire place. "I have to tell Maddie a couple of things, things I can only tell her in front of her family and friends. First, everything in my life has changed since you entered it, Maddie Leaver. And I mean *everything*. I was like a lost little puppy before I met you. In these last few months, everything has gone right for me. Every *fucking* thing, excuse my French. And I can trace it all back to you. Maddie, you are the light in my life. I want you to know that. I want everyone here to know that. And that's why I want to do this on stage in view of everyone gathered here."

Before any of us can begin to guess what he's doing, Axel gets on one knee.

And he pulls out a ring.

And now we can guess what he's doing.

"Maddie Leaver," he says, a slight tremor in his voice betraying a hidden nervousness. "Will you marry me?"

My brother's girlfriend starts to cry. She raises her hand to her mouth and nods.

She can't stop nodding.

"Yes, Axel. *Yes*."

And, just like that, the entire party erupts into applause and a very loud whoop from Drake and Bishop comes from the back of the room as Axel joyously and tenderly fits the ring onto Maddie's finger.

I must say I'm crying too. She looks so happy.

*My brother's done something good and something smart, for once.*

I turn to find Mom in the crowd, desiring to see her reaction to all this. She's standing next to Winston, who's clapping. Mom has tears running down her face, just like me.

I am so glad she's here to see this.

Axel's actually managed to find a good girl and make her his fiancée.

*Yep. Pigs really should be able to fly now.*

The members of Ravaged rush the stage before any of us. They envelop Axel and Maddie in a big hug, which makes me laugh and cry with happiness. There is so much love in the room. Bishop, Caspian, and Drake all hug Axel so much and so hard that he starts to protest.

"I can't breathe!"

They continue to squeeze the life out of him, though.

The rest of the party all gather around Maddie. I love the ring my brother's given her. She shows it off between her tears.

"You didn't tell me about this," I say to Axel in an accusatory tone.

"I didn't tell anyone," he replies with a wink. "Well, maybe I told one or two people..."

"Like who?"

*Ah.*

I spin around to Bishop.

"You knew about this?" I ask him, incandescent that my man's been hiding this clandestine operation.

He shrugs. "A member of Ravaged can't hide a secret from another member. And besides, I couldn't trust you wouldn't have let something slip while you were drunk with Maddie."

Axel laughs.

*God, both of them are so infuriating.*

I check out Maddie's ring. "It's beautiful," I say. She

seems like she's in shock. She can't stop smiling and crying at the same time.

And then Mom appears. She wraps her arms around Maddie.

"Welcome to the family, Maddie. Properly this time."

"Thank you, Astrid. Thank you for everything."

"You're going to be an amazing daughter-in-law. What do you think, Chloe?"

"For sure. I wholeheartedly agree."

They break the hug and Maddie subtly tilts her head in the direction of Winston on the other side of the room.

"What were you two talking about?" she asks Mom slyly. Even in the chaos of being engaged, she's still trying to figure out if her plan worked or not.

"Wouldn't you two like to know?" Mom asks, giving us both the side-eye.

"Well, you were having a long chat with him," I say, raising an eyebrow.

Mom sighs, knowing she's lost this battle. "We're going to meet up tomorrow..."

"A date?" Maddie interjects, still animated about her party's hidden agenda even if she's just been proposed to.

"Nothing fancy," Mom replies. "And maybe nothing will happen. We're just catching up, that's all."

"Sounds like a date," Maddie says to me. I wink back in agreement. Mom is not amused.

The boys of Ravaged decide they want to toast Axel and Maddie. We all raise our glasses as Drake leads.

"To the newest official member of Ravaged," the lead singer says, gesturing towards Maddie. "Welcome."

We all cheer.

Maddie goes to dry her tears. Mom speaks with Axel. And everyone disperses. The party continues.

And that's when Bishop leans over me from behind. I

feel his hands sneakily reach down my lower back towards my ass.

"I'm horny," he whispers into my ear.

*Oh, I really shouldn't...*

But it's very hard to turn him down. Impossible, in fact. Especially when his deep voice drips into my ear like that and I can feel his desire for me.

"Maybe I can do something about that," I whisper back.

His hand finds mine, and then he's leading me secretly away from the party. Everyone has gone back into their own conversations by now, so there isn't any suspicion. Music is playing on the loudspeakers. No one is going to miss us for ten minutes, right?

*Right?*

Bishop takes me into one of the bathrooms in the house. As he locks the door, I lock eyes with him.

"Just like how we used to have to sneak around as teenagers," I remark.

"I always thought I'd get caught," Bishop replies.

I giggle. "Shut up and fuck me, Bishop."

He lowers the toilet lid and sits down on it, inviting me closer with just a flick of his finger.

"Pull out my cock," he orders.

I unzip his fly and lower the zipper until his erection is revealed. I take in a breath, still amazed after all this time at the sight of his manhood.

I look up at the man, desperate for what he wants from me next.

"Strip down and ride me," he commands in a deep voice.

I don't say a word. I pull down my dress and panties so that I'm completely naked. I climb on top of him and lower myself onto his shaft. My eyes roll back and I let out a strangled cry as he fills me. I rock against him as Bishop grunts.

His hands massage my breasts. Pinching my nipples between his index finger and thumb. Turning me on just by those rough hands of his.

He's so warm. My heart flutters as he grips my bare ass to support me as we move together. Bringing out the bliss.

I gasp. Once. Twice.

The feel of him...

The authority...

I'm crazed.

We're doing this here... in my brother's house...

"So naughty," I whisper to the man.

"You're being so bad," he replies. "I couldn't resist you. Chloe, you're a bad influence on me."

"I am? What about you? I can't stop thinking about you."

"Shut up and let me fuck you."

He pumps in deep inside. I let out another cry, quickly covering my mouth. Afraid of someone over-hearing us.

I feel like such a little slut, and I'm loving it. My breasts hang loose, bouncing freely in Bishop's face. He admires them with unrestrained glee.

I catch a glimpse of us in the bathroom mirror.

"Oh, fuck," I whisper. "We are so bad."

"Worse than teenagers," Bishop replies.

The rockstar glares at me with intensity in his eyes. He grabs at my hair from behind, yanking my head back in one glorious tug.

My mouth hangs open as I ride him into blissful oblivion.

I shudder against him as I feel his legs vibrate.

"Come for me," I whisper. "Fuck me hard. You're such a bad boy."

Bishop grunts and unloads his load inside me. I lean

back and take him in, feeling like such a bad girl doing it here like this.

*Oh, it turns me on...*

# 47

*CHLOE*

"Where have you guys been?" Axel asks us both as Bishop and I walk back down the hallway towards the living room. My brother's standing at the doorway just before you get into the party with his arms crossed like an angry school principal and we've two troublemakers.

I freeze in his headlights. I would not want Axel, in a million years, to know what we were just doing in that bathroom.

But Bishop doesn't even flinch.

"Just exploring this lovely house of yours," he replies to his bandmate.

"Hm." Axel eyes us both suspiciously as we pass him back into the party. I feel Bishop's hand on my lower back guiding me through the doorway. He smiles at Axel.

*Remind me never to get in the middle of a fight between those two men.*

Maddie skips over to us. She wraps her arm around Axel's.

"Come," she says. "We're all heading out to a bar to celebrate tonight. Let's get a drink."

I look at Bishop. He's still smiling.

"Sounds great," I reply.

And so we follow the rest of the party out the front door of the house.

Bishop's hand remains on my lower back, sending shivers down my spine. He's so possessive of me. It really makes my heart giddy.

And that's when the impulse hits me.

I turn back to my man and get him to lean towards me with a flick of my finger. He obeys my command willingly. I speak into his ear the words I should've said a long time ago.

"I love you, Bishop."

He doesn't say it back.

Instead of the words I long to hear, he says something else.

"I've got an idea."

"What?" I ask him, afraid of what he means by that.

This time Bishop leans in even further so that his lips are brushing my ear.

"Let's get married."

I let out a snort. "You're joking."

But his face isn't joking.

"How about we get married tonight, Chloe?"

"What?"

I feel like a broken record repeating myself.

*What? What? What?*

My whole world is flipping upside down.

*Marriage? Tonight?*

"Let's go to Vegas right now and just fucking do it," he continues, as if he isn't clinically insane. "I've waited seven years for you, girl. I think, Chloe, it's fair to say you are the love of my life. Why should we wait any longer for something we know is the right thing to do?"

"Bishop..."

"Marry me," he says in his deepest and most confident voice. "Right now, Chloe Stoll."

I blink.

Despite the whiplash this is all giving me, it seems right. Too right.

And then I find myself uttering the word *yes*.

"Yes, I'll marry you, Bishop."

My man – my brand-new *fiancé* – whistles at Axel and Maddie to come over. My hands start trembling as my brother and his own brand new fiancée make their way towards us, but Bishop finds my hand and squeezes it for the hundredth time tonight, forcing my nerves still.

"Sorry to steal your thunder tonight, Axel," Bishop says to my brother. "But I've just asked your sister to marry me. Tonight."

Both Maddie and Axel stare at us both in shock.

"And you said yes?" my brother asks me.

I can't even speak. I just nod.

There's complete silence as we all, except for Bishop, try to comprehend what's happening.

"Well," Maddie says, breaking the tension. "Then what are we waiting for?"

*If I've only got this one life*
*It's you I'll spend it with*
*Yeah, with you I'll live my forever*

*The storms may come*
*And batter our roof*
*We may try and we may fail*
*Life might throw nightmares at us*

*But if I've got you next to me*
*Then this life will be the greatest*
*Yeah, the greatest life I could live*

# 48

*BISHOP*

I JUST KNOW I have to marry Chloe Stoll, so why bother taking the time? Tonight is as good a night as any.

I'm afraid my sudden, impulsive decision to drop everything and wed the girl of my life would make the others feel like I'm overshadowing Maddie and Axel's night, but Astrid's reaction to the news only makes me understand what I'm doing is the right thing.

"Of course," she says when we tell her the plan. "You two are *meant* to be together. Gosh, this is so exciting."

"So, you're not mad?" I ask her.

"Mad? Why would I be mad? Tonight, my little family has suddenly doubled, no mother would be mad at that."

Instead of going out with the party, we all change course.

We call Lucas. The manager who can fix any problem.

Axel rings him, tells him that he and Maddie are engaged, and then hands the phone to me.

"One more thing..." I tell Lucas about my proposal to Chloe and how it has to be tonight.

"Vegas?" he asks, already guessing our plans.

"Yep. Vegas."

"You want me to get the private jet fired up?"

I check the time. "It's still early in the night," I reply, turning to the rest of the group. All the boys of Ravaged are around me, waiting for my next move. Astrid and Maddie are standing side by side. Tonight has been a good night so far. The best night. How about I keep things going? I look at my bride-to-be. She's smiling. Her shocked - but elated - face when I told her that I want to marry her is the highlight of everything so far. I want to make tonight special. For her. "How about you get the tour bus and swing it by here," I suggest to Lucas. "I'm up for a little road trip."

Soon enough, Lucas turns up outside of Axel and Maddie's with Ravaged's tour bus. The name of our band is printed in bright colors along the side of it. He parks it on our driveway and welcomes us all in.

"You are crazy, Bishop, you know that?" Lucas greets me as I board the bus. He slaps me on the shoulder.

"Yeah, but that's why you love me, right?"

"You've got me there."

Chloe follows behind.

"And you're crazy for marrying this asshole," Lucas tells her.

My girl beams back at him. "Maybe I am, but I wouldn't have it any other way."

Lucas laughs.

Chloe turns around and gestures towards her room-mate. "Lucas, meet my friend Gary. He's been amazing these last few days."

The two men shake hands, and I see something fly between them. A little spark, perhaps?

I knew something like that would happen, hence why I mentioned my manager to Gary earlier at the party.

*Ha. Here goes.*

"Hi," Lucas says to the big man.

Gary's eyes fly up and down the body of Ravaged's manager. "Hello, gorgeous."

*Oh, yes. Here we go...*

Good for Lucas. Too long he's been busy taking care of us boys he's barely had any time to live his own life. Maybe Gary might be the guy to loosen him up.

As she steps on the bus, Chloe winks at me. Lucas and Gary are stuck talking to each other. Already hitting it off.

"You're such a cupid," I whisper to her.

"I'm just introducing my friends," she replies with a mock-innocent, high-pitched voice. "If they *like like* each other, then that's down to them."

I roll my eyes and take a seat.

We get to Vegas in the early morning. The bus ride is so fun. We play classic tunes and have a proper singalong. Lucas made sure the bus' supply of champagne was full before he rode it to us, so we have a great time in the back.

This is the rockstar life. Being surrounded by your closest friends and family. Rocking out. Celebrating being alive, our successes, and our relationships.

It's the best night of our lives.

Only one thing spoils it.

Drake.

At some point in the ride, he corners me in the back of the bus so that we're alone together.

"I don't like it," he says with a serious-looking frown on his pretty face.

I roll my eyes. I know Drake well enough to know what he's saying. Us boys in Ravaged are closer than brothers and can practically finish each other's sentences.

"What don't you like, Drake?"

"Axel, and now you..."

"Now us, *what?*"

The lead singer of Ravaged shrugs. "You two are obsessed with girls. This isn't what the band's about. The band is the most important thing."

"The band's not losing out just because two of us have found our happiness," I retort. I'm getting annoyed at my bandmate's insistence. Sure, we did come up with rules that forbade anything else, especially relationships, to become more important than the band, but Chloe... Maddie... they're different. They're not just some *girls* us two rockstars have picked up for shits and giggles. Chloe is the love of my life, always has been. And Maddie is Axel's love.

"We should be practicing," Drake continues darkly. "Not going to Vegas."

I face up to my brother. "Shut up, Drake, and just enjoy this moment."

Drake grumbles and leans back in his seat. "Okay."

But there is an ominous look about him I don't like.

I pat him on the shoulder and join the others. He spends some time wallowing in the back of the bus before he steps back into the celebrations with a smile on his face, putting the gloomy conversation behind him. Where it should be.

We don't stop once we arrive in Las Vegas. We head straight to the nearest chapel and get ourselves married. The girls in our group all rush off to get Chloe as ready as she can be in twenty minutes, while us boys make sure the service will go as planned.

Of course, Drake and Caspian are my best men. They make a great show of it by immediately buying us boys a round of shots to do together.

"You can't get married being sober," Drake tells me. "You're a freaking rockstar. That would be heresy."

"Trust me," I reply. "I am *far* from sober."

"You're really going to do this?" Axel asks me, placing a firm hand on my shoulder. "You're going to marry my sister?"

I nod. Seriously. "Yep."

"And you're going to treat her right?"

I nod again. "Yes. More than anything in the world."

My bandmate stares me deep in my eyes before he too nods.

"Then you have my blessing, Bishop."

He leaves to find his sister as the rest of us take our places in the chapel. The rest of the girls come in. Maddie raises two thumbs up at me as if to say *this is really fucking happening*, and Astrid slyly shakes her head when she sees me.

And then the music starts.

It's Chloe's choice.

Landslide by Fleetwood Mac.

*Of course. Why would we even play anything different?*

The opening verse of the song echoes through the chapel as my bride enters.

And she is beautiful. Radiant.

Like always.

And the most amazing thing about her – the thing that makes me light up like fireworks and realize that marrying her is the best decision of my life – is her smile when she sees me.

We are so in love that it's *gross*.

Axel walks her down the aisle, taking her arm. Brother and sister. That's what makes Astrid start to cry.

"I can't believe we're actually doing this," Chloe mouths to me as she stands beside me.

"You still want to do this?" I whisper back.

She looks up at me with those eyes I've fallen in love with a thousand times. "Yes, more than anything else."

\* \* \*

AFTER THE WEDDING, we are all so incredibly hungry. We're drunk, we've just rode on a bus from LA to Vegas, we've experienced a billion different emotions in one night, and it's now early morning... Of course we are starving.

We stumble to the nearest restaurant from the chapel.

But someone is waiting outside for us.

The last person any of us wants to see.

Caspian is the first one to spot him. "Harold," he growls as he sees the paparazzo standing on the street outside the chapel.

None of us have time to react before the "journalist" raises his expensive-ass professional camera and takes a blinding photo of us.

"What the fuck?" Axel lets go of his fiancée's hand and approaches Harold. "This is a private occasion. What the fuck are you doing here?"

Harold smiles, knowing he's already got the shot he was here to get. "I followed you here from LA. It's always good to get a Ravaged photo, especially when you're all in it at your most vulnerable."

"Leave," I say to the man, gently guiding my new wife protectively behind me.

Drake steps forward by my side. "Fuck off, Harold."

He's saying what we're all thinking.

But the paparazzo merely strokes his chin in a deliberately obnoxious attempt to piss us off. "I was saying to myself on the way here... *why* would Ravaged suddenly go to Vegas?" he asks rhetorically. "Someone must be getting married. A little shotgun wedding, perhaps?"

His gaze zooms in on Maddie and her engagement ring. He smiles. He is lapping this up like a cat and a bowl of milk.

He then quickly raises his camera a second time, physically pushing past Axel to take a photo of his fiancée.

*Snap.*

"I'm going to be the first person in the country to break this story," the man says self-congratulatory.

"Back the fuck away from my pregnant fiancée," Axel says, his voice trembling as he tries to restrain himself.

He realizes, too late, that he's said the wrong thing.

Harold smiles.

He looks at the rest of us. Then at Maddie.

Specifically, her pregnant belly. Ravaged's secret we're keeping from the world.

"How perfect," he whispers excitedly. "The best story to break. She's not only getting married, but she's also *pregnant.*"

And then he leans forward, pressing his camera mere inches from her face.

The act is so aggressive. So forceful.

And then there's a yell. A guttural roar.

It's coming from Caspian.

The man barges past Maddie and punches Harold right in the jaw, making the photographer collapse instantly to the ground.

Knocked out.

Caspian stops.

"Fuck," he says.

We're all silent.

In shock.

*Did Caspian really just full-on punch the man?*

Drake kneels down and checks Harold's heartbeat.

"He's okay," our lead singer says. "He's still breathing. Just unconscious. We'll need to call an ambulance, though."

Caspian sits down in despair.

Chloe takes my hand.

Axel looks around at all of us. "Shit," he says, the situation finally dawning. "This is going to be big fucking news."

# 49

SEVEN YEARS AGO

*BISHOP*

My heart is broken over Chloe Stoll, but I hide it well.

I hide it from Drake Sharpe as he tells us about this band he wants to create.

I hide it from Caspian Ford, the band's new drummer.

And I especially hide it from Axel Stoll. He and I have had our war of words. Our fight over his sister that came to blows – and a black eye on my end - and now we've come to a truce.

But I still haven't healed my heart.

She hates me now. Chloe Stoll will always hate me.

And I've got to live with that to pursue this dream.

One day, when I am super rich and famous and living far away from here in some big mansion, I'll swoop on back to Crystal River and impress the girl. Maybe then she'll forget and forgive the past.

*Maybe.*

"We're going to do this right," Drake says. We're all standing in his parents' garage, our instruments ready. Ravaged's first practice session. "I have serious aspirations for us. We could get big someday. We could make real money from this. We could live our lives doing what we love. But we've got to work hard, and we've got to take this seriously, and we've got to make Ravaged the most important thing in our lives."

We all nod in agreement.

We're all on the same page.

We want to make it big.

"No hard drugs," Drake continues. "We've got to stay focused on the music. *Die* doing the music. I want you to swear by it."

"I swear," Caspian growls.

"I swear," Axel says, looking at me. There's still a touch of animosity there, but I know it'll pass in time.

Drake's laser-like attention turns to me.

"I swear," I say.

"And I swear," Drake says. "In fact, let's set up some rules before we play our first note. Number one, in order to not get distracted, no long-term girls..."

# EPILOGUE

*CHLOE*

We're all back at Axel and Maddie's place, debating what our next moves are going to be.

As he came to after Caspian's wild punch, we all took Harold to the nearest hospital and left him in their care, making sure any health expenses go straight to us. We didn't know what else to do. The man's fine, by the way. Caspian knocked him the fuck out but didn't kill him.

Truthfully, I'm surprised that Harold hasn't been punched like that before, but this is Caspian we're talking about. The man is built to take on the heavyweight champion of the world, so that one punch was more than enough.

Lucas is the one typically bringing order back to the situation. "Caspian punching that asshole is going to come out on the news tomorrow," he says somberly. "The police will probably get involved, but I'm pretty confident I can talk them out of pressing charges. They know who Harold is. They know who we are."

"Shit," Bishop says under his breath. He squeezes my

hand. He's not let it go since the incident. All the way back to Los Angeles.

I still can't get over the fact we're now husband and wife, despite how crazy tonight has turned out to be. Honestly, I wouldn't take back a thing, and I know Bishop doesn't either. He told me the exact same when we were on the bus coming back.

"The publicity around this is not going to be good," Lucas continues. "Real bad. As you all know, Harold is one of the top paparazzi in this town, and his connections are wide. Even if he doesn't press charges and this isn't a criminal matter, he'll still pursue this through the media. That's what he wants to do. I bet he's already got dollar signs in his eyes as we speak, the asshole. The man is known to hold a solid grudge, and he'll never shy away from making an easy buck. I just want to warn you all that this is really going to be bad."

Gary is by his side. "You really know what you're doing, huh?" he remarks. "You're the real brains behind Ravaged."

Lucas smiles back.

*Oh shit. There really are sparks flying between the two now.*

My little cupid plan, like Maddie's, seems to have worked.

Lucas' phone rings.

"This is important," he says. "I've got to take this."

He leaves the room.

Now it's Drake's turn to speak. "This punch is definitely not going to be a good image for the band."

"We can handle it," Bishop replies.

"I agree," Axel adds.

"How are you feeling, Maddie?" I ask my friend.

Axel's fiancée nods sadly. "I was pretty shocked by that

camera being pushed up against me. I hope he hasn't still got the photo."

That made me so furious. The fact that the man thought it was perfectly fine to invade her space and her privacy like that, especially when she's pregnant. At least she's okay. But it does make me worried about what I've signed up for being both Bishop's wife and also my own music career...

Axel sighs. "We'll figure that out when it comes to it, I guess."

"Yep."

"You okay, Caspian?" Bishop asks. The man has been characteristically silent since coming back. He's not even said a word. Damn, he must be going through hell right now. Bishop knows him so well and told me on the bus that he'll be feeling like all this is his fault for a single moment of aggression. I know he's spent his whole life trying to not let that side of him out, so what's just happened would be so painful for the guy.

He's the loyal one of the band. The most honorable. This must be eating him up inside.

Caspian doesn't respond. His face is unreadable. Stony. I notice his knuckles are white. There's a fire burning inside that man, and he's doing everything to keep it hidden from the rest of us.

He's in pain.

Lucas steps back into the room. "That was Harold's lawyer on the phone," he says. The whole room goes silent. "My prediction was right. The police can't do shit, but he's preparing to sue and also publish everything in the tabloids. He's also got photos of Maddie. It's going to come down hard on us. We've got to prepare ourselves for what's to come."

And then Caspian speaks. The whole room goes silent as Ravaged's drummer opens his mouth.

"I'm going to take some time off."

"From what?" Bishop asks.

"From Ravaged," Caspian replies. "I've ruined everything because of who I am, and I've got to pay the price. I'm going to lie low. I can't bring down the band because of my actions. You can find another drummer. Someone who won't destroy what we've made. Like the rules we made when we started, this is a distraction. *I* am a distraction. I need to leaven before I ruin everything else."

And then he turns around and walks straight out of the house.

I call out his name. So does Maddie. So do Axel and Bishop and Drake.

But Caspian doesn't stop.

He leaves without looking back.

Drake turns around to the rest of us.

"Where the hell is he going?"

WANT to read what happens next?

Go to rebeccacastle.com to find the links for Ravaged From Fate (Ravaged Rockstars III)

# ABOUT THE AUTHOR

Rebecca has had the storytelling bug since... forever!

What Rebecca likes most is writing steamy hot filthy romances with sweet happy endings sprinkled with some delicious bad boys.

Born and raised in an Aussie coastal town, she loves travelling around the world - meeting new people and discovering their stories.

Aside from adventuring she also enjoys a good rainy day in with a good book or at a hot beach catching the sun.

She's a world-class napping professional. You'll most likely find her asleep snuggled up on a sofa somewhere cozy.

For other titles and information please visit
rebeccacastle.com

facebook.com/rebeccacastleauthor
instagram.com/rebeccacastle.author